The Colors of Space

The Colors of Space

by Marion Zimmer Bradley

Start Publishing PD is a registered trademark of Start Publishing PD LLC
Manufactured in the United States of America

Cover art: Shutterstock/Taisiya Kozorez

Cover design: Jennifer Do

10 9 8 7 6 5 4 3 2 1

ISBN 979-8-8809-1401-2

Table of Contents

Chapter One

The Lhari spaceport didn't belong on Earth.

Bart Steele had thought that, a long time ago, when he first saw it. He had been just a kid then; twelve years old, and all excited about seeing Earth for the first time—Earth, the legendary home of mankind before the Age of Space, the planet of Bart's far-back ancestors. And the first thing he'd seen on Earth, when he got off the starship, was the Lhari spaceport.

And he'd thought, right then, It doesn't belong on Earth.

He'd said so to his father, and his father's face had gone strange, bitter and remote.

"A lot of people would agree with you, Son," Captain Rupert Steele had said softly. "The trouble is, if the Lhari spaceport wasn't on Earth, we wouldn't be on Earth either. Remember that."

Bart remembered it, five years later, as he got off the strip of moving sidewalk. He turned to wait for Tommy Kendron, who was getting his baggage off the center strip of the moving roadway. Bart Steele and Tommy Kendron had graduated together, the day before, from the Space Academy of Earth. Now Tommy, who had been born on the ninth planet of the star Capella, was taking the Lhari starship to his faraway home, and Bart's father was coming back to Earth, on the same starship, to meet his son.

Five years, Bart thought. That's a long time. I wonder if Dad will know me?

"Let me give you a hand with that stuff, Tommy."

"I can manage," Tommy chuckled, hefting the plastic cases. "They don't allow you much baggage weight on the Lhari ships. Certainly not more than I can handle."

The two lads stood in front of the spaceport gate for a minute. Over the gate, which was high and pointed and made of some clear colorless material like glass, was a jagged symbol resembling a flash of lightning; the sign, in Lhari language, for the home world of the Lhari.

They walked through the pointed glass gate, and stood for a moment, by mutual consent, looking down over the vast expanse of the Lhari spaceport.

This had once been a great desert. Now it was all floored in with some strange substance that was neither glass, metal nor concrete; it looked like gleaming crystal—though it felt soft underfoot—and in the glare of the noonday sun, it gave back the glare in a million rainbow flashes. Tommy put his hands up to his eyes to shield them. "The Lhari must have funny eyes, if they can stand all this glare!"

Inside the glass gate, a man in a guard's uniform gave them each a pair of dark glasses. "Put them on now, boys. And don't look directly at the ship when it lands."

Tommy hooked the earpieces of the dark glasses over his ears, and sighed with relief. Bart frowned, but finally put them on. Bart's mother had been a Mentorian—from the planet Mentor, of the star Deneb, a hundred times brighter than the sun. Bart had her eyes. But Mentorians weren't popular on Earth, and Bart had learned to be quiet about his mother.

Through the dark lenses, the glare was only a pale gleam. Far out in the very center of the spaceport, a high, clear-glass skyscraper rose, catching the sunlight in a million colors. Around the building, small copters and robotcabs veered, discharging passengers; and the moving sidewalks were crowded with people coming and going. Here and there in the crowd, standing out because of their height and the silvery metallic cloaks they wore, were the strange tall figures of the Lhari.

"Well, how about going down?" Tommy glanced impatiently at his timepiece. "Less than half an hour before the starship touches down."

"All right. We can get a sidewalk over here." Reluctantly, Bart tore his eyes from the fascinating spectacle, and followed Tommy, stepping onto one of the sidewalks. It bore them down a long, sloping ramp toward the floor of the spaceport, then sped toward the glass skyscraper; came to rest at the wide pointed doors, depositing them in the midst of the crowd. The jagged lightning flash was there over the doors of the building, and the words:

here, by grace of the Lhari, is the doorway to all the stars.

Bart remembered, as if it were yesterday, how he and his father had first passed through this doorway. And his father, looking up, had said under his breath "Not for always, Son. Someday men will have a doorway to the stars, and the Lhari won't be standing in the door."

Inside the building, it was searingly bright. The high open rotunda was filled with immense mirrors, and glass ramps running up and down, moving staircases, confusing signs and flashing lights on tall oddly shaped pillars. The place was crowded with men from all over the planet, but the dark glasses they all wore gave them a strange sort of family resemblance.

Tommy said, "I'd better check my reservations."

Bart nodded. "Meet you on the upper level later," he said, and got on a moving staircase that soared slowly upward, past level after level, toward the information desk located on the topmost mezzanine.

The staircase moved slowly, and Bart had plenty of time to see everything. On the step immediately in front of him, two Lhari were standing; with their backs turned, they might almost have been men. Unusually tall, unusually thin, but men. Then Bart amended that mentally. The Lhari had two arms, two legs and a head apiece—they were that much like men. Their faces had two eyes, two ears, and a nose and mouth, all in the right places. But the similarity ended there.

They had skin of a curious pale silvery gray, and pale, pure-white hair rising in what looked like a feathery crest. The eyes were long and slanting, the forehead high and narrow, the nose delicately thin and chiseled with long vertically slit nostrils, the ears long, pointed and lobeless. The mouth looked almost human, though the chin was abnormally pointed. The hands would almost have passed inspection as human hands—except for the long, triangular nails curved over the fingertips like the claws of a cat. They wore skin-tight clothes of some metallic silky stuff, and long flowing gleaming silvery capes. They looked unearthly, elfin and strange, and in their own way they were beautiful.

The two Lhari in front of Bart had been talking softly, in their fast twittering speech; but as the hum of the crowds on the upper levels grew louder, they raised their voices, and Bart could hear what they were saying. He was a little surprised to find that he could still understand the Lhari language. He hadn't heard a word of it in years—not since his Mentorian mother died. The Lhari would never guess that he could understand their speech. Not one human in a million could speak or understand a dozen words of Lhari, except the Mentorians.

"Do you really think that human—" the first Lhari spoke the word as if it were a filthy insult—"will have the temerity to come in by this ship?"

"No reasonable being can tell what humans will do," said the second Lhari. "But then, no reasonable being can tell what our own Port Authorities will do either! If the message had only reached us sooner, it would have been easier. Now I suppose it will have to clear through a dozen officials and a dozen different kinds of formalities."

The younger Lhari sounded angry. "And we have only a description—no name, nothing! How do they expect us to do anything under those conditions? What I can't understand is how it ever happened, or how the man managed to get away. What worries me is the possibility that he may have communicated with others we don't know about. Those bungling fools who let the first man get away can't even be sure—"

"Do not speak of it here," said the old Lhari sharply. "There are Mentorians in the crowd who might understand us." He turned and looked straight at Bart, and Bart felt as if the slanted strange eyes were looking right through to his bones. The Lhari said, in Universal, "Who are you, boy? What iss your businessses here?"

Bart replied in the same language, politely, "My father's coming in on this ship. I'm looking for the information desk."

"Up there," said the old Lhari, pointing with a clawed hand, and lost interest in Bart. He said to his companion, in their own language, "Always, I regret these episodes. I have no malice against humans. I suppose even this Vegan that we are seeking has young, and a mate, who will regret his loss."

"Then he should not have pried into Lhari matters," said the younger Lhari fiercely. "If they'd killed him right away—"

The soaring staircase swooped up to the top level; the two Lhari stepped off and mingled swiftly with the crowd, being lost to sight. Bart whistled in dismay as he got off and turned toward the information desk. A Vegan! Some poor guy from his own planet was in trouble with the Lhari. He felt a cold, crawling chill down his insides. The Lhari had spoken regretfully, but the way they'd speak of a fly they couldn't manage to swat fast enough. Sooner or later you had to get down to it, they just weren't human!

Here on Earth, nothing much could happen, of course. They wouldn't let the Lhari hurt anyone—then Bart remembered his course in Universal Law. The Lhari spaceport in every system, by treaty, was Lhari territory. Once you walked beneath the lightning-flash sign, the authority of the planet ceased to function; you might as well be on that unbelievably remote world in another galaxy that was the Lhari home planet—that world no human had ever seen. On a Lhari spaceport, or on a Lhari ship, you were under the jurisdiction of Lhari law.

Tommy stepped off a moving stair and joined him. "The ship's on time—it reported past Luna City a few minutes ago. I'm thirsty—how about a drink?"

There was a refreshment stand on this level; they debated briefly between orange juice and a drink with a Lhari name that meant simply cold sweet, and finally decided to try it. The name proved descriptive; it was very cold, very sweet and indescribably delicious.

"Does this come from the Lhari world, I wonder?"

"I imagine it's synthetic," Bart said.

"I suppose it won't hurt us?"

Bart laughed. "They wouldn't serve it to us if it would. No, men and Lhari are alike in a lot of ways. They breathe the same air. Eat about the same food." Their bodies were adjusted to about the same gravity. They had the same body chemistry—in fact, you couldn't tell Lhari blood from human, even under a microscope. And in the terrible Orion Spaceport wreck sixty years ago, doctors had found that blood plasma from humans could be used for wounded Lhari, and vice versa, though it wasn't safe to transfuse whole blood. But then, even among humans there were five blood types.

And yet, for all their likeness, they were different.

Bart sipped the cold Lhari drink, seeing himself in the mirror behind the refreshment stand; a tall teen-ager, looking older than his seventeen years. He was lithe and well muscled from five years of sports and acrobatics at the Space Academy, he had curling red hair and gray eyes, and he was almost as tall as a Lhari.

Will Dad know me? I was just a little kid when he left me here, and now I'm grown-up.

Tommy grinned at him in the mirror. "What are you going to do, now we've finished our so-called education?"

"What do you think? Go back to Vega with Dad, by Lhari ship, and help him run Vega Interplanet. Why else would I bother with all that astrogation and math?"

"You're the lucky one, with your father owning a dozen ships! He must be almost as rich as the Lhari."

Bart shook his head. "It's not that easy. Space travel inside a system these days is small stuff; all the real travel and shipping goes to the Lhari ships."

It was a sore point with everyone. Thousands of years ago, men had spread out from Earth—first to the planets, then to the nearer stars, crawling in ships that could travel no faster than the speed of light. They had even believed that was an absolute limit—that nothing in the universe could exceed the speed of light. It took years to go from Earth to the nearest star.

But they'd done it. From the nearer stars, they had sent out colonizing ships all through the galaxy. Some vanished and were never heard from again, but some made it, and in a few centuries man had spread all over hundreds of star-systems.

And then man met the people of the Lhari.

It was a big universe, with measureless millions of stars, and plenty of room for more than two intelligent civilizations. It wasn't surprising that the Lhari, who had only been traveling space for a couple of thousand years themselves, had never come across humans before. But they had been delighted to meet another intelligent race—and it was extremely profitable.

Because men were still held, mostly, to the planets of their own star-systems. Ships traveling between the stars by light-drive were rare and ruinously expensive. But the Lhari had the warp-drive, and almost overnight the whole picture changed. By warp-drive, hundreds of times faster than light at peak, the years-long trip between Vega and Earth, for instance, was reduced to about three months, at a price anyone could pay. Mankind could trade and travel all over their galaxy, but they did it on Lhari ships. The Lhari had an absolute, unbreakable monopoly on star travel.

"That's what hurts," Tommy said. "It wouldn't do us any good to have the star-drive. Humans can't stand faster-than-light travel, except in cold-sleep."

Bart nodded. The Lhari ships traveled at normal speeds, like the regular planetary ships, inside each star-system. Then, at the borders of the vast gulf of emptiness between stars, they went into warp-drive; but first, every human on board was given the cold-sleep treatment that placed them in suspended animation, allowing their bodies to endure the warp-drive.

He finished his drink. The increasing bustle in the crowds below them told him that time must be getting short. A tall, impressive-looking Lhari strode through the crowd, followed at a respectful distance by two Mentorians, tall, redheaded humans wearing metallic cloaks like those of the Lhari. Tommy nudged Bart, his face bitter.

"Look at those lousy Mentorians! How can they do it? Fawning upon the Lhari that way, yet they're as human as we are! Slaves of the Lhari!"

Bart felt the involuntary surge of anger, instantly controlled. "It's not that way at all. My mother was a Mentorian, remember. She made five cruises on a Lhari ship before she married my father."

Tommy sighed. "I guess I'm just jealous—to think the Mentorians can sign on the Lhari ship as crew, while you and I will never pilot a ship between the stars. What did she do?"

"She was a mathematician. Before the Lhari met up with men, they used a system of mathematics as clumsy as the old Roman numerals. You have to admire them, when you realize that they learned stellar navigation with their old system, though most ships use human math now. And of course, you know their eyes aren't like ours. Among other things, they're color-blind. They see everything in shades of black or white or gray.

"So they found out that humans aboard their ships were useful. You remember how humans, in the early days in space, used certain birds, who were more sensitive to impure air than they were. When the birds keeled over, they could tell it was time for humans to start looking over the air systems! The Lhari use Mentorians to identify colors for them. And, since Mentor was the first planet of humans that the Lhari had contact with, they've always been closer to them."

Tommy looked after the two Mentorians enviously. "The fact is, I'd ship out with the Lhari myself if I could. Wouldn't you?"

Bart's mouth twisted in a wry smile. "No," he said. "I could—I'm half Mentorian, I can even speak Lhari."

"Why don't you? I would."

"Oh, no, you wouldn't," Bart said softly. "Not even very many Mentorians will. You see, the Lhari don't trust humans too much. In the early days, men were always planting spies on Lhari ships, to try and steal the secret of warp-drive. They never managed it, but nowadays the Lhari give all the Mentorians what amounts to a brainwashing—deep hypnosis, before and after every voyage, so that they can neither look for anything that might threaten the Lhari monopoly of space, nor reveal it—even under a truth drug—if they find it out.

"You have to be pretty fanatical about space travel to go through that. Oh, my mother could tell us a lot of things about her cruises with the Lhari. The Lhari can't tell a diamond from a ruby, except by spectrographic analysis, for instance. And she—"

A high gong note sounded somewhere, touching off an explosion of warning bells and buzzers all over the enormous building. Bart looked up.

"The ship must be coming in to land."

"I'd better check into the passenger side," Tommy said. He stuck out his hand. "Well, Bart, I guess this is where we say good-bye."

They shook hands, their eyes meeting for a moment in honest grief. In some indefinable way, this parting marked the end of their boyhood.

"Good luck, Tom. I'm going to miss you."

They wrung each other's hands again, hard. Then Tommy picked up his luggage and started down a sloping ramp toward an enclosure marked TO PASSENGER ENTRANCE.

Warning bells rang again. The glare intensified until the glow in the sky was unendurable, but Bart looked anyhow, making out the strange shape of the Lhari ship from the stars.

It was huge and strange, glowing with colors Bart had never seen before. It settled down slowly, softly: enormous, silent, vibrating, glowing; then swiftly faded to white-hot, gleaming blue, dulling down through the visible spectrum to red. At last it was just gleaming glassy Lhari-metal color again. High up in the ship's side a yawning gap slid open, extruding stairsteps, and men and Lhari began to descend.

Bart ran down a ramp and surged out on the field with the crowd. His eyes, alert for his father's tall figure, noted with surprise that the ship's stairs were guarded by four cloaked Lhari, each with a Mentorian interpreter. They were stopping each person who got off the starship, asking for identity papers. Bart realized he was seeing another segment of the same drama he had overheard discussed, and wished he knew what it was all about.

The crowd was thinning now. Robotcabs were swerving in, hovering above the ground to pick up passengers, then veering away. The gap in the starship's side was closing, and still Bart had not seen the tall, slim, flame-haired figure of his father. The port on the other side of the ship, he knew, was for loading passengers. Bart moved carefully through the thinning crowd, almost to the foot of the stairs. One of the Lhari checking papers stopped and fixed him with an inscrutable gray stare, but finally turned away again.

Bart began really to worry. Captain Steele would never miss his ship! But he saw only one disembarking passenger who had not yet been surrounded by a group of welcoming relatives, or summoned a robotcab and gone. The man was wearing Vegan clothes, but he wasn't Bart's father. He was a fat little man, with ruddy cheeks and a fringe of curling gray hair all around his bald dome. Maybe he'd know if there was another Vegan on the ship.

Then Bart realized that the little fat man was staring straight at him. He returned the man's smile, rather hesitantly; then blinked, for the fat man was coming straight toward him.

"Hello, Son," the fat man said loudly. Then, as two of the Lhari started toward him, the strange man did an incredible thing. He reached out his two hands and grabbed Bart.

"Well, boy, you've sure grown," he said, in a loud, cheerful voice, "but you're not too grown-up to give your old Dad a good hug, are you?" He pulled Bart roughly into his arms. Bart started to pull away and stammer that the fat man had made a mistake, but the pudgy hand gripped his wrist with unexpected strength.

"Bart, listen to me," the stranger whispered, in a harsh fast voice. "Go along with this or we're both dead. See those two Lhari watching us? Call me Dad, good and loud, if you want to live. Because, believe me, your life's in danger—right now!"

Chapter Two

For a moment, pulled off balance in the fat stranger's hug, Bart remained perfectly still, while the man repeated in that loud, jovial voice, "How you've grown!" He let him go, stepping away a pace or two, and whispered urgently, "Say something. And take that stupid look off your face."

As he stepped back, Bart saw his eyes. In the chubby, good-natured red face, the stranger's eyes were half-mad with fear.

In a split second, Bart remembered the two Lhari and their talk of a fugitive. In that moment, Bart Steele grew up.

He stepped toward the man and took him quickly by the shoulders.

"Dad, you sure surprised me," he said, trying to keep his voice from shaking. "Been such a long time, I'd—half forgotten what you looked like. Have a good trip?"

"About like always." The fat man was breathing hard, but his voice sounded firm and cheerful. "Can't compare with a trip on the old Asterion though." The Asterion was the flagship of Vega Interplanet, Rupert Steele's own ship. "How's everything?"

Beads of sweat were standing out on the man's ruddy forehead, and his grip on Bart's wrist was so hard it hurt. Bart, grasping at random for something to say, gabbled, "Too bad you couldn't get to my graduation. I made th-third in a class of four hundred—"

The Lhari had surrounded them and were closing in.

The fat man took a deep breath or two, said, "Just a minute, Son," and turned around. "You want something?"

The tallest of the Lhari—the old one, whom Bart had seen on the escalator—looked long and hard at him. When they spoke Universal, their voices were sibilant, but not nearly so inhuman.

"Could we trrrouble you to sssshow us your paperrrssss?"

"Certainly." Nonchalantly, the fat man dug them out and handed them over. Bart saw his father's name printed across the top.

The Lhari gestured to a Mentorian interpreter: "What colorrr isss thisss man's hairrr?"

The Mentorian said in the Lhari language, "His hair is gray." He used the Universal word; there were, of course, no words for colors in the Lhari speech.

"The man we sssseek has hair of red," said the Lhari. "And he isss tall, not fat."

"The boy is tall and with red hair," the Mentorian volunteered, and the old Lhari made a gesture of disdain.

"This boy is twenty years younger than the man whose description came to us. Why did they not give us a picture or at least a name?" He turned to the other Lhari and said in their own shrill speech, "I suspected this man because he was alone. And I had seen this boy on the upper mezzanine and spoken with him. We watched him, knowing sooner or later the father would seek him. Ask him." He gestured and the Mentorian said, "Who is this man, you?"

Bart gulped. For the first time he noted the energon-ray shockers at the belts of the four Lhari. He'd heard about those. They could stun—or they could kill, and quite horribly. He said, "This is my father. You want my cards, too?" He hauled out his identity papers. "My name's Bart Steele."

The Lhari, with a gesture of disgust, handed them back. "Go, then, father and son," he said, not unkindly.

"Let's get going, Son," said the little bald man. His hand shook on Bart's, and Bart thought, If we're lucky, we can get out of the port before he faints dead away. He said "I'll get a copter," and then, feeling sorry for the stranger, gave him his arm to lean on. He didn't know whether he was worried or scared. Where was his father? Why did this man have his dad's papers? Was his father hiding inside the Lhari ship? He wanted to run, to burst away from the imposter, but the guy was shaking so hard Bart couldn't just leave him standing there. If the Lhari got him, he was a dead duck.

A copter swooped down, the pilot signaling. The little man said hoarsely, "No. Robotcab."

Bart waved the copter away, getting a dirty look from the pilot, and punched a button at the stand for one of the unmanned robotcabs. It swung down, hovered motionless. Bart boosted the fat man in. Inside, the man collapsed on the seat, leaning back, puffing, his hand pressed hard to his chest.

"Punch a combo for Denver," he said hoarsely.

Bart obeyed, automatically. Then he turned on the man.

"It's your game, mister! Now tell me what's going on? Where's my father?"

The man's eyes were half-shut. He said, gasping, "Don't ask me any questions for a minute." He thumbed a tablet into his mouth, and presently his breathing quieted.

"We're safe—for the minute. Those Lhari would have cut us down."

"You, maybe. I haven't done anything. Look, you," Bart said in sudden rage, "you owe me some explanations. For all I know, you're a criminal and the Lhari have every right to chase you! Why have you got my father's papers? Did you steal them to get away from the Lhari? Where's my father?"

"It's your father they were looking for, you young fool," said the man, gasping hard. "Lucky they had only a description and not a name—but they've probably got that by now, uncoded. We've only confused them for a little while. But if you hadn't played along, they'd have had you watched, and when they get hold of the name Steele—they will, sooner or later, the people in the Procyon system—"

"Where is my father?"

"I hope I don't know," the fat man said. "If he's still where I left him, he's dead. My name is Briscoe. Edmund Briscoe. Your father saved my life years ago, never mind how. The less you know, the safer you'll be for a while. His major worry just now is about you. He was afraid, if he didn't turn up here, you'd take the first ship back to Vega. So he gave me his papers and sent me to warn you—"

Bart shook his head. "It all sounds phony as can be. How do I know whether to believe you or not?" His hand hovered over the robotcab controls. "We're going straight to the police. If you're okay, they won't turn you over to the Lhari. If you're not—"

"You young fool," said the fat man, with feeble violence, "there's no time for all that! Ask me questions—I can prove I know your father!"

"What was my mother's name?"

"Oh, God," Briscoe said, "I never saw her. I knew your father long before you were born. Until he told me, I never knew he'd married or had a son. I'd never have known you, except that you're the living image—" He shook his head helplessly, and his breathing sounded hoarse.

"Bart, I'm a sick man, I'm going to die. I want to do what I came here to do, because your father saved my life once when I was young and healthy, and gave me twenty good years before I got old and fat and sick. Win or lose, I won't live to see you hunted down like a dog, like my own son—"

"Don't talk like that," Bart said, a creepy feeling coming over him. "If you're sick, let me take you to a doctor."

Briscoe did not even hear. "Wait, there is something else. Your father said, 'Tell Bart I've gone looking for the Eighth Color. Bart will know what I mean.'"

"That's crazy. I don't know—"

He broke off, for the memory had come, full-blown:

He was very young: five, six, seven. His mother, tall and slender and very fair, was bending over a blueprint, pointing with a delicate finger at something, straightening, saying in her light musical voice:

"The fuel catalyst—it's a strange color, a color you never saw anywhere. Can you think of a color that isn't red, orange, yellow, green, blue, violet, indigo or some combination of them? It isn't any of the colors of the spectrum at all. The fuel is a real eighth color."

And his father had used the phrase, almost adopted it. "When we know what the eighth color is, we'll have the secret of the star-drive, too!"

Briscoe saw his face change, nodded weakly. "I see it means something to you. Now will you do as I tell you? Within a couple of hours, they'll be combing the planet for you, but by that time the ship I came in on will have taken off again. They only stop a short time here, for mail, passengers—no cargo. They may get under way again before all messages are cleared and decoded." He stopped and breathed hard. "The Earth authorities might protect you, but you would never be able to board a Lhari ship again—and that would mean staying on Earth for the rest of your life. You've got to get away before they start comparing notes. Here." His hand went into his pockets. "For your hair. It's a dye—a spray."

He pressed a button on the bulb in his hand; Bart gasped, feeling cold wetness on his head. His own hand came away stained black.

"Keep still." Briscoe said irritably. "You'll need it at the Procyon end of the run. Here." He stuck some papers into Bart's hand, then punched some buttons on the robotcab's control. It wheeled and swerved so rapidly that Bart fell against the fat man's shoulder.

"Are you crazy? What are you going to do?"

Briscoe looked straight into Bart's eyes. In his hoarse, sick voice, he said, "Bart, don't worry about me. It's all over for me, whatever happens. Just remember this. What your father is doing is worth doing, and if you start stalling, arguing, demanding explanations, you can foul up a hundred people—and kill about half of them."

He closed Bart's fingers roughly over the papers. The robotcab hovered over the spaceport. "Now listen to me, very carefully. When I stop the cab, down below, jump out. Don't stop to say good-bye, or ask questions, or anything else. Just get out, walk straight through the passenger door and straight up the ramp of the ship. Show them that ticket, and get on. Whatever happens, don't let anything stop you. Bart!" Briscoe shook his shoulder. "Promise! Whatever happens, you'll get on that ship!"

Bart swallowed, feeling as if he'd been shoved into a silly cops-and-robbers game. But Briscoe's urgency had convinced him. "Where am I going?"

"All I have is a name—Raynor Three," Briscoe said, "and the message about the Eighth Color. That's all I know." His mouth twisted again in that painful gasp.

The cab swooped down. Bart found his voice. "But what then? Is Dad there? Will I know—"

"I don't know any more than I've told you," Briscoe said. Abruptly the robotcab came to a halt, swaying a little. Briscoe jerked the door open, gave Bart a push, and Bart found himself stumbling out on the ramp beside the spaceport building. He caught his balance, looked around, and realized that the robotcab was already climbing the sky again.

Immediately before him, neon letters spelled TO PASSENGER ENTRANCE ONLY. Bart stumbled forward. The Lhari by the gate thrust out a disinterested claw. Bart held up what Briscoe had shoved into his hand, only now seeing that it was a thin wallet, a set of identity papers and a strip of pink tickets.

"Procyon Alpha. Corridor B, straight through." The Lhari gestured, and Bart went through the narrow passageway, came out at the other end, and found himself at the very base of a curving stair that led up and up toward a door in the side of the huge Lhari ship. Bart hesitated. In another minute he'd be on his way to a strange sun and a strange world, on what might well be the wild-goose chase of all time.

Passengers were crowding the steps behind him. Someone shouted suddenly, "Look at that!" and someone else yelled, "Is that guy crazy?"

Bart looked up. A robotcab was swooping over the spaceport in wild, crazy circles, dipping down, suddenly making a dart like an enraged wasp at a little nest of Lhari. They ducked and scattered; the robotcab swerved away, hovered, swooped back. This time it struck one of the Lhari grazingly with landing gear and knocked him sprawling. Bart stood with his mouth open, as if paralyzed.

Briscoe! What was he doing?

The fallen Lhari lay without moving. The robotcab moved in again, as if for the kill, buzzing viciously overhead.

Then a beam of light arced from one of the drawn energon-ray tubes. The robotcab glowed briefly red, then seemed to sag, sink together; then puddled, a slag heap of molten metal, on the glassy floor of the port. A little moan of horror came from the crowd, and Bart felt a sudden, wrenching sickness. It had been like a game, a silly game of cops and robbers, and suddenly it was as serious as melted death lying there on the spaceport. Briscoe!

Someone shoved him and said, "Come on, quit gawking, kid. They won't hold the ship all day just because some nut finds a new way to commit suicide."

Bart, his legs numb, walked up the ramp. Briscoe had died to give him this chance. Now it was up to him to make it worth having.

Chapter Three

At the top of the ramp, a Lhari glanced briefly at his papers, motioned him through. Bart passed through the airlock, and into a brightly lit corridor half full of passengers. The line was moving slowly, and for the first time Bart had a chance to think.

He had never seen violent death before. In this civilized world, you didn't. He knew if he thought about Briscoe, he'd start bawling like a baby, so he swallowed hard a couple of times, set his chin, and concentrated on the trip to Procyon Alpha. That meant this ship was outbound on the Aldebaran run—Proxima Centauri, Sirius, Pollux, Procyon, Capella and Aldebaran.

The line of passengers was disappearing through a doorway. A woman ahead of Bart turned and said nervously, "We won't be put into cold-sleep right away, will we?"

He reassured her, remembering his inbound trip five years ago. "No, no. The ship won't go into warp-drive until we're well past Pluto. It will be several days, at least."

Beyond the doorway the lights dwindled, and a Mentorian interpreter took his dark glasses, saying, "Kindly remove your belt, shoes and other accessories of leather or metal before stepping into the decontamination chamber. They will be separately decontaminated and returned to you. Papers, please."

With a small twinge of fright, Bart surrendered them. Would the Mentorian ask why he was carrying two wallets? Inside the other one, he still had his Academy ID card which identified him as Bart Steele, and if the Mentorian looked through them to check, and found out he was carrying two sets of identity papers....

But the Mentorian merely dumped all his pocket paraphernalia, without looking at it, into a sack. "Just step through here."

Holding up his trousers with both hands, Bart stepped inside the indicated cubicle. It was filled with faint bluish light. Bart felt a strong tingling and a faint electrical smell, and along his forearms there was a slight prickling where the small hairs were all standing on end. He knew that the invisible R-rays were killing all the microorganisms in his body, so that no disease germ or stray fungus would be carried from planet to planet.

The bluish light died. Outside, the Mentorian gave him back his shoes and belt, handed him the paper sack of his belongings, and a paper cup full of greenish fluid.

"Drink this."

"What is it?"

The medic said patiently, "Remember, the R-rays killed all the microorganisms in your body, including the good ones—the antibodies that protect you against disease, and the small yeasts and bacteria that live in your intestines and help in the digestion of your food. So we have to replace those you need to stay healthy. See?"

The green stuff tasted a little brackish, but Bart got it down all right. He didn't much like the idea of drinking a solution of "germs," but he knew that was silly. There was a big difference between disease germs and helpful bacteria.

Another Mentorian official, this one a young woman, gave him a key with a numbered tag, and a small booklet with WELCOME ABOARD printed on the cover.

The tag was numbered 246-B, which made Bart raise his eyebrows. B class was normally too expensive for Bart's father's modest purse. It wasn't quite the luxury class A, reserved for planetary governors and ambassadors, but it was plenty luxurious. Briscoe had certainly sent him traveling in style!

B Deck was a long corridor with oval doors; Bart found one numbered 246, and, not surprisingly, the key opened it. It was a pleasant little cabin, measuring at least six feet by eight, and he would evidently have it to himself. There was a comfortably big bunk, a light that could be turned on and off instead of the permanent glow-walls of the cheaper class, a private shower and toilet, and a placard on the walls informing him that passengers in B class had the freedom of the Observation Dome and the Recreation Lounge. There was even a row of buttons dispensing synthetic foods, in case a passenger preferred privacy or didn't want to wait for meals in the dining hall.

A buzzer sounded and a Mentorian voice announced, "Five minutes to Room Check. Passengers will please remove all metal in their clothing, and deposit in the lead drawers. Passengers will please recline in their bunks and fasten the retaining straps before the steward arrives. Repeat, passengers will please...."

Bart took off his belt, stuck it and his cuff links in the drawer and lay down. Then, in a sudden panic, he got up again. His papers as Bart Steele were still in the sack. He got them out, and with a feeling as if he were crossing a bridge and burning it after him, tore up every scrap of paper that identified him as Bart Steele of Vega Four, graduate of the Space Academy of Earth. Now, for better or worse, he was—who was he? He hadn't even looked at the new papers Briscoe had given him!

He glanced through them quickly. They were made out to David Warren Briscoe, of Aldebaran Four. According to them, David Briscoe was twenty years old, hair black, eyes hazel, height six foot one inch. Bart wondered, painfully, if Briscoe had a son and if David Briscoe knew where his father was. There was also a license, validated with four runs on the Aldebaran Intrasatellite Cargo Company—planetary ships—with the rank of Apprentice Astrogator; and a considerable sum of money.

Bart put the papers in his pants pocket and the torn-up scraps of his old ones into the trashbin before he realized that they looked exactly like what they were—torn-up legal identity papers and a broken plastic card. Nobody destroyed identity papers for any good reason. What could he do?

Then he remembered something from the Academy. Starships were closed-system cycles, no waste was discarded, but everything was collected in big chemical tanks, broken down to separate elements, purified and built up again into new materials. He threw the paper into the toilet, worked the plastic card back and forth, back and forth until he had wrenched it into inch-wide bits, and threw it after them.

The cabin door opened and a Mentorian said irritably, "Please lie down and fasten your straps. I haven't all day."

Hastily Bart flushed the toilet and went to the bunk. Now everything that could identify him as Bart Steele was on its way to the breakdown tanks. Before long, the complex hydrocarbons and cellulose would all be innocent little molecules of carbon, oxygen, hydrogen; they might turn up in new combinations as sugar on the table!

The Mentorian grumbled, "You young people think the rules mean everybody but you," and strapped him far too tightly into the bunk. Bart felt resentful; just because Mentorians could work on Lhari ships, did they have to act as if they owned everybody?

When the man had gone, Bart drew a deep breath. Was he really doing the right thing?

If he'd refused to get out of the robotcab—

If he'd driven Briscoe straight to the police—

Then maybe Briscoe would still be alive. And now it was too late.

A warning siren went off in the ship, rising to hysterical intensity. Bart thought, incredulously, this is really happening. It felt like a nightmare. His father a fugitive from the Lhari. Briscoe dead. He himself traveling, with forged papers, to a star he'd never seen.

He braced himself, knowing the siren was the last warning before takeoff. First there would be the hum of great turbines deep in the ship, then the crushing surge of acceleration. He had made a dozen trips inside the solar system, but no matter how often he did it, there was the strange excitement, the little pinpoint of fear, like an exotic taste, that was almost pleasant.

The door opened and Bart grabbed a fistful of bed-ticking as two Lhari came into the room.

One of them said, in their strange shrill speech, "This boy is the right age."

Bart froze.

"You're seeing spies in every corner, Ransell," said the other, then in Universal, "Could we trrouble you for your paperesses, sirr?"

Bart, strapped down and helpless, moved his head toward the drawer, hoping his face did not betray his fear. He watched the two Lhari riffle through his papers with their odd pointed claws.

"What isss your planet?"

Bart bit his lip, hard—he had almost said, "Vega Four."

"Aldebaran Four."

The Lhari said in his own language, "We should have Margil in here. He actually saw them."

The other replied, "But I saw the machine that disintegrated. I still say there was enough protoplasm residue for two bodies."

Bart fought to keep his face perfectly straight.

"Did anyone come into your cabin?" The Lhari asked in Universal.

"Only the steward. Why? Is something wrong?"

"There iss some thought that a stowaway might be on boarrd. Of courrrse we could not allow that, anyone not prrroperly prrotected would die in the first shift into warp-drive."

"Just the steward," Bart said again. "A Mentorian."

The Lhari said, eying him keenly, "You are ill? Or discommoded?"

Bart grasped at random for an excuse. "That—that stuff the medic made me drink made me feel—sort of sick."

"You may send for a medical officer after acceleration," said the Lhari expressionlessly. "The summoning bell is at your left."

They turned and went out and Bart gulped. Lhari, in person, checking the passenger decks! Normally you never saw one on board; just Mentorians. The

Lhari treated humans as if they were too dumb to bother about. Well, at least for once someone was acting as if humans were worthy antagonists. We'll show them—someday!

But he felt very alone, and scared....

A low hum rose, somewhere in the ship, and Bart grabbed ticking as he felt the slow surge. Then a violent sense of pressure popped his ear drums, weight crowded down on him like an elephant sitting on his chest, and there was a horrible squashed sensation dragging his limbs out of shape. It grew and grew. Bart lay still and sweated, trying to ease his uncomfortable position, unable to move so much as a finger. The Lhari ships hit 12 gravities in the first surge of acceleration. Bart felt as if he were spreading out, under the weight, into a puddle of flesh—melted flesh like Briscoe's—

Bart writhed and bit his lip till he could taste blood, wishing he were young enough to bawl out loud.

Abruptly, it eased, and the blood started to flow again in his numbed limbs. Bart loosened his straps, took a few deep breaths, wiped his face—wringing wet, whether with sweat or tears he wasn't sure—and sat up in his bunk. The loudspeaker announced, "Acceleration One is completed. Passengers on A and B Decks are invited to witness the passing of the Satellites from the Observation Lounge in half an hour."

Bart got up and washed his face, remembering that he had no luggage with him, not so much as a toothbrush.

At the back of his mind, packed up in a corner, was the continuing worry about his father, the horror at Briscoe's ghastly death, the fear of the Lhari; but he slammed the lid firmly on them all. For the moment he was safe. They might be looking for Bart Steele by now, but they weren't looking for David Briscoe of Aldebaran. He might just as well relax and enjoy the trip. He went down to the Observation Lounge.

It had been darkened, and one whole wall of the room was made of clear quartzite. Bart drew a deep breath as the vast panorama of space opened out before him.

They were receding from the sun at some thousands of miles a minute. Swirling past the ship, gleaming in the reflected sunlight like iron filings moving to the motion of a magnet, were the waves upon waves of cosmic dust—tiny free electrons, ions, particles of gas; free of the heavier atmosphere, themselves invisible, they formed in their billions into bright clouds around the ship; pale, swirling veils of mist. And through their dim shine, the brilliant flares of the fixed stars burned clear and steady, so far away that even the hurling motion of the ship could not change their positions.

One by one he picked out the constellations. Aldebaran swung on the pendant chain of Taurus like a giant ruby. Orion strode across the sky, a swirling nebula at his belt. Vega burned, cobalt blue, in the heart of the Lyre.

Colors, colors! Inside the atmosphere of Earth's night, the stars had been pale white sparks against black. Here, against the misty-pale swirls of cosmic dust, they burned with color heaped on color; the bloody burning crimson of Antares, the metallic gold of Capella, the sullen pulsing of Betelgeuse. They burned, each with its own inward flame and light, like handfuls of burning jewels flung by some giant hand upon the swirling darkness. It was a sight Bart felt he could watch forever and still be hungry to see; the never-changing, ever-changing colors of space.

Behind him in the darkness, after a long time, someone said softly, "Imagine being a Lhari and not being able to see anything out there but bright or brighter light."

A bell rang melodiously in the ship and the passengers in the lounge began to stir and move toward the door, to stretch limbs cramped like Bart's by tranced watching, to talk quickly of ordinary things.

"I suppose that bell means dinner," said a vaguely familiar voice at Bart's elbow. "Synthetics, I suppose, but at least we can all get acquainted."

The light from the undarkened hall fell on their faces as they moved toward the door. "Bart! Why, it can't be!"

In utter dismay, Bart looked down into the face of Tommy Kendron.

In the rush of danger, he had absolutely forgotten that Tommy Kendron was on this ship—to make his alias useless; Tommy was looking at him in surprise and delight.

"Why didn't you tell me, or did you and your father decide at the last minute? Hey, it's great that we can go part way together, at least!"

Bart knew he must cut this short very quickly. He stepped out into the full corridor light so that Tommy could see his black hair.

"I'm sorry, you're confusing me with someone else."

"Bart, come off it—" Tommy's voice died out. "Sorry, I'd have sworn you were a friend of mine."

Bart wondered suddenly, had he done the wrong thing? He had a feeling he might need a friend. Badly.

Well, it was too late now. He stared Tommy in the eye and said, "I've never seen you before in my life."

Tommy looked deflated. He stepped back slightly, shaking his head. "Never saw such a resemblance. Are you a Vegan?"

"No," Bart lied flatly. "Aldebaran. David Briscoe."

"Glad to know you, Dave." With undiscourageable friendliness, Tommy stuck out a hand. "Say, that bell means dinner, why don't we go down together? I don't know a soul on the ship, and it looks like luck—running into a fellow who could be my best friend's twin brother."

Bart felt warmed and drawn, but sensibly he knew he could not keep up the pretense. Sooner or later, he'd give himself away, use some habitual phrase or gesture Tommy would recognize.

Should he take a chance—reveal himself to Tommy and ask him to keep quiet? No. This wasn't a game. One man was already dead. He didn't want Tommy to be next.

There was only one way out. He said coldly, "thank you, but I have other things to attend to. I intend to be very busy all through the voyage." He spun on his heel and walked away before he could see Tommy's eager, friendly smile turn hurt and defensive.

Back in his cabin, he gloomily dialed some synthetic jellies, thinking with annoyance of the anticipated good food of the dining room. He knew he couldn't risk meeting Tommy again, and drearily resigned himself to staying in his cabin. It looked like an awfully boring trip ahead.

It was. It was a week before the Lhari ship went into warp-drive, and all that time Bart stayed in his cabin, not daring to go to the observation Lounge or dining hall. He got tired of eating synthetics (oh, they were nourishing enough, but they were altogether uninteresting) and tired of listening to the tapes the room steward got him from the ship's library. By the time they had been in space a week, he was so bored with his own company that even the Mentorian medic was a welcome sight when he came in to prepare him for cold-sleep.

Bart had had the best education on Earth, but he didn't know precisely how the Lhari warp-drive worked. He'd been told that only a few of the Lhari understood it, just as the man who flew a copter didn't need to understand Newton's Three Laws of Motion in order to get himself back and forth to work.

But he knew this much; when the ship generated the frequencies which accelerated it beyond the speed of light, in effect the ship went into a sort of fourth dimension, and came out of it a good many light-years away. As far as Bart knew, no human being had ever survived warp-drive except in the suspended animation which they called cold-sleep. While the medic was professionally reassuring him and strapping him in his bunk, Bart wondered what humans would do with the Lhari star-drive if they had it. Well, he supposed they could use automation in their ships.

The Mentorian paused, needle in hand. "Do you wish to be wakened for the week we shall spend in each of the Proxima, Sirius and Pollux systems, sir? You can, of course, be given enough drug to keep you in cold-sleep until we reach the Procyon system."

Bart wondered if the room steward had mentioned the passenger so bored with the trip that he didn't even visit the Observation Lounge. He felt tempted—he was getting awfully tired of staring at the walls. On the other hand, he wanted very much to see the other star-systems. When he passed through them on the trip to Earth, he'd been too young to pay much attention.

Firmly he put the temptation aside. Better not to risk meeting other passengers, Tommy especially, if he decided he couldn't take the boredom.

The needle went into his arm. He felt himself sinking into sleep, and, in sudden panic, realized that he was helpless. The ship would touch down on three worlds, and on any of them the Lhari might have his description, or his alias! He could be taken off, drugged and unconscious, and might never wake up! He tried to move, to protest, to tell them he was changing his mind, but already he was unable to speak. There was a freezing moment of intense, painful cold. Then he was floating in what felt like waves of cosmic dust, swirling many-colored before his eyes. And then there was nothing, no color, nothing at all except the nowhere night of sleep.

Chapter Four

Bart felt cold. He stirred, moved his head in drowsy protest; then memory came flooding back, and in sudden panic he sat up, flinging out his arms as if to ward away anyone who would lay hands on him.

"Easy!" said a soothing voice. A Mentorian—not the same Mentorian—bent over him. "We have just entered the gravitational field of Procyon planet Alpha, Mr. Briscoe. Touchdown in four hours."

Bart mumbled an apology.

"Think nothing of it. Quite a number of people who aren't used to the cold-sleep drug suffer from minor lapses of memory. How do you feel now?"

Bart's legs were numb and his hands tingled when he sat up; but his body processes had been slowed so much by the cold-sleep that he didn't even feel hungry; the synthetic jelly he'd eaten just before going to sleep wasn't even digested yet.

When the Mentorian left for another cabin, Bart looked around, and suddenly felt he would stifle if he stayed here another minute. He wasn't likely to run into Tommy twice in a row, and if he did, well, Tommy would probably remember the snub he'd had and stay away from Dave Briscoe. And he wanted another sight of the stars—before he went into worry and danger.

He went down to the Observation Lounge.

The cosmic dust was brighter out here, and the constellations looked a little flattened. Textbook tables came back to him. He had traveled 47 light-years—he couldn't remember how many billions of miles that was. Even so, it was only the tiniest hop-skip-and-jump in the measureless vastness of space.

The ship was streaking toward Procyon, a sol-type star, bright yellow; the three planets, Alpha, Beta and Gamma, ringed like Saturn and veiled in shimmering layers of cloud, swung against the night. Past them other stars, brighter stars, faraway stars he would never see, glimmered through the pale dust....

"Hello, Dave. Been space-sick all this time? Remember me? I met you about six weeks ago in the lounge down here—just out from Earth."

Oh, no! Bart turned, with a mental groan, to face Tommy. "I've been in cold-sleep," he said. He couldn't be rude again.

"What a dull way to face a long trip!" Tommy said cheerily. "I've enjoyed every minute of it myself."

It was hard for Bart to realize that, for Tommy, their meeting had been six weeks ago. It all seemed dreamlike. The closer he came to it, the less he could realize that in a few hours he'd be getting off on a strange world, with only the strange name Raynor Three as a guide. He felt terribly alone, and having Tommy close at hand helped, even though Tommy didn't know he was helping.

"Maybe I should have stayed awake."

"You should," Tommy said. "I only slept for a couple of hours at each warp-drive shift. We had a day-long stopover at Sirius Eighteen, and I took a tour of the planet. And I've spent a lot of time down here, just star-gazing—not that it did me much good. Which one is Antares? How do you tell it from Aldebaran? I'm always getting them mixed up."

Bart pointed. "Aldebaran—that's the big red one there," he said. "Think of the constellation Taurus as a necklace, with Aldebaran hanging from it like a locket. Antares is much further down in the sky, in relation to the arbitrary sidereal axis, and it's a deeper red. Like a burning coal, while Aldebaran is like a ruby—"

He broke off in mid-word, realizing that Tommy was gazing at him in a mixture of triumph and consternation. Too late, Bart realized he had been tricked. Studying for an exam, the year before, he had explained the difference between the two red stars in almost the same words.

"Bart," Tommy said in a whisper, "I knew it had to be you. Why didn't you tell me, fella?"

Bart felt himself start to smile, but it only stretched his mouth. He said, very low, "Don't say my name out loud Tom. I'm in terrible trouble."

"Why didn't you tell me? What's a friend for?"

"We can't talk here. And all the cabins are wired for sound in case somebody stops breathing, or has a heart attack in space," Bart said, glancing around.

They went and stood at the very foot of the quartz window, seeming to tread the brink of a dizzying gulf of cosmic space, and talked in low tones while Alpha and Beta and Gamma swelled like blown-up balloons in the port.

Tommy listened, almost incredulous. "And you're hoping to find your father, with no more information than that? It's a big universe," he said, waving at the gulf of stars. "The Lhari ships, according to the little tourist pamphlet they gave me, touch down at nine hundred and twenty-two different stars in this galaxy!"

Bart visibly winced, and Tommy urged, "Come to Capella with me. You can stay with my family as long as you want to, and appeal to the Interplanet authority to find your father. They'd protect him against the Lhari, surely. You can't chase all over the galaxy playing interplanetary spy all by yourself, Bart!"

But Briscoe had deliberately gone to his death, to give Bart the chance to get away. He wouldn't have died to send Bart into a trap he could easily have sprung on Earth.

"Thanks, Tommy. But I've got to play it my way."

Tommy said firmly, "Count me in then. My ticket has stopover privileges. I'll get off at Procyon with you."

It was a temptation—to have a friend at his back. He put his hand on Tommy's shoulder, grateful beyond words. But fresh horror seized him as he remembered the horrible puddle of melted robotcab with Briscoe somewhere in the residue. Protoplasm residue enough for two bodies. He couldn't let Tommy face that.

"Tommy, I appreciate that, believe me. But if I did find my father and his friends, I don't want anyone tracing me. You'd only make the danger worse. The best thing you can do is stay out of it."

Tommy faced him squarely. "One thing's for sure. I'm not going to let you go off and never know whether you're alive or dead."

"I'll try to get a message to you," Bart said, "if I can. But whatever happens, Tommy, stay with the ship and go on to Capella. It's the one thing you can do to help me."

A warning bell rang in the ship. He broke sharply away from Tommy, saying over his shoulder, "It's all you can do to help, Tom. Do it—please? Just stay clear?"

Tommy reached out and caught his arm. "Okay," he said reluctantly, "I will. But you be careful," he added fiercely. "You hear me? And if I don't hear from you in some reasonable time, I'll raise a stink from here to Vega!"

Bart broke away and ran. He was afraid, if he didn't, he'd break up again. He closed the cabin door behind him, trying to calm down so that the Mentorian steward, coming to strap him in for deceleration, wouldn't see how upset he was. He was going to need all his nerve.

He went through another decontamination chamber, and finally moved, with a line of passengers, out of the yawning airlock, under the strange sun, into the strange world.

At first sight it was a disappointment. It was a Lhari spaceport that lay before him, to all appearances identical with the one on Earth: sloping glass ramps, tall colorless pylons, a skyscraper terminus crowded with men of all planets. But the sun overhead was brilliant and clear gold, the shadows sharp and violet on the spaceport floor. Behind the confines of the spaceport he could see the ridges of tall hills and unfamiliarly colored trees. He longed to explore them, but he got a grip on his imagination, surrendering his ticket stub and false papers to the Lhari and Mentorian interpreter who guarded the ramp.

The Lhari said to the Mentorian, in the Lhari language, "Keep him for questioning but don't tell him why." Bart felt a cold chill icing his spine. This was it.

The Mentorian said briefly, "We wish to check on the proper antibody component for Aldebaran natives. There will be a delay of about thirty minutes. Will you kindly wait in this room here?"

The room was comfortable, furnished with chairs and a vision-screen with some colorful story moving on it, small bright figures in capes, curious beasts racing across an unusual veldt; but Bart paced the floor restlessly. There were two doors in the room. Through one of them, he had been admitted; he could see, through the glass door, the silhouette of the Mentorian outside. The other door was opaque, and marked in large letters:

DANGER HUMANS MUST NOT PASS WITHOUT SPECIAL LENSES TYPE X. ORDINARY SPACE LENSES WILL NOT SUFFICE DANGER! LHARI OPENING! ADJUST X LENSES BEFORE OPENING!

Bart read the sign again. Well, that was no way out, for sure! He had heard that the Lhari sun was almost 500 times as bright as Earth's. The Mentorians alone, among humans, could endure Lhari lights—he supposed the warning was for ordinary spaceport workers.

A sudden, rather desperate plan occurred to Bart. He didn't know how much light he could tolerate—he'd never been on Mentor—but he had inherited some of his mother's tolerance for light. And blindness would be better than being burned down with an energon-gun! He went hesitantly toward the door, and pushed it open.

His eyes exploded into pain; automatically his hands went up to shield them. Light, light—he had never known such cruelly glowing light. Even through the lids there was pain and red afterimages; but after a moment, opening them a slit, he found that he could see, and made out other doors, glass ramps, pale Lhari figures coming and going. But for the moment he was alone in the long corridor beyond which he could see the glass ramps.

Nearby, a door opened into a small office with glass walls; on a peg, one of the silky metallic cloaks worn by Mentorians doing spaceport work was hanging. On an impulse, Bart caught it up and flung it around his shoulders.

It felt cool and soft, and the hood shielded his eyes a little. The ramp leading down to what he hoped was street level was terribly steep and there were no steps. Bart eased himself over the top of the ramp and let go. He whooshed down the slick surface on the flat of his back, feeling the metal of the cloak heat with the friction, and came to a breathless jarring stop at the bottom. Whew, what a slide! Three stories, at least! But there was a door, and outside the door, maybe, safety.

A voice hailed him, in Lhari. "You, there!"

Bart could see well now. He made out the form of a Lhari, only a colorless blob in the intense light.

"You people know better than to come back here without glasses. Do you want to be blinded, my friend?" He actually sounded kind and concerned. Bart tensed, his heart pounding. Now that he was caught, could he bluff his way out? He hadn't actually spoken the Lhari language in years, though his mother had taught it to him when he was young enough to learn it without a trace of accent.

Well, he must try. "Margil sent me to check," he improvised quickly. "They were holding someone for questioning, and he seems to have gotten away somehow, so I wanted to make sure he didn't come through here."

"What is the matter that one man can give us all the slip this way?" the Lhari said curiously. "Well, one thing is sure, he's Vegan or Solarian or Capellan, one of the dim-star people. If he comes through here, we'll catch him easily enough while he's stumbling around half blind. You know that you shouldn't stay long." He gestured. "Out this way—and don't come back without special lenses."

Bart nodded, jerking the cloak around his shoulders, forcing himself not to break into a run as he stepped through the door the Lhari indicated. It closed behind him. Bart blinked, feeling as if he had stepped into pitch darkness. Only slowly did his eyes adapt and he became aware that he was standing in a city street, in the full glow of Procyon sunlight, and apparently outside the Lhari spaceport entirely.

He'd better get to cover! He took off the Mentorian cloak, thrust it under his arm. He raised his eyes, which were adjusting to ordinary light again, and stopped dead.

Just across the street was a long, low, rainbow colored building. And the letters—Bart blinked, thinking his eyes deceived him—spelled out:
EIGHT COLORS TRANSSHIPPING CORPORATION
CARGO, PASSENGERS, MESSAGES, EXPRESS
A. RAYNOR ONE, MANAGER

Chapter Five

For a moment the words swirled before Bart's still-watering eyes. He wiped them, trying to steady himself. Had he so soon reached the end of his dangerous quest? Somehow he had expected it to lie in deep, dark concealment.

Raynor One. The existence of Raynor One presupposed a Raynor Two and probably a Raynor Three—for all he knew, Raynors Four, Five, Six, and Sixty-six! The building looked solid and real. It had evidently been there a long time.

With his hand on the door, he hesitated. Was it, after all, the right Eight Colors? But it was a family saying; hardly the sort of thing you'd be apt to hear outside. He pushed the door and went in.

The room was filled with brighter light than the Procyon sun outdoors, the edges of the furniture rimmed with neon in the Mentorian fashion. A prim-looking girl sat behind a desk—or what should have been a desk, except that it looked more like a mirror, with little sparkles of lights, different colors, in regular rows along one edge. The mirror-top itself was blue-violet and gave her skin and her violet eyes a bluish tinge. She was smooth and lacquered and glittering and she raised her eyebrows at Bart as if he were some strange form of life she hadn't seen very often.

"I'd—er—like to see Raynor One," he said.

Her dainty pointed fingernail, varnished blue, stabbed at points of light. "On what business?" she asked, not caring.

"It's a personal matter."

"Then I suggest you see him at his home."

"It can't wait that long."

The girl studied the glassy surface and punched at some more of the little lights. "Name, please?"

"David Briscoe."

He had thought her perfect-painted face could not show any emotion except disdain, but it did. She looked at him in open, blank consternation. She said into the vision-screen, "He calls himself David Briscoe. Yes, I know.

Yes, sir, yes." She raised her face, and it was controlled again, but not bored. "Raynor One will see you. Through that door, and down to the end of the hall."

At the end of the hallway was another door. He stepped through into a small cubicle, and the door slid shut like a closing trap. He whirled in panic, then subsided in foolish relief as the cubicle began to rise—it was just an automatic elevator.

It rose higher and higher, stopping with an abrupt jerk, and slid open into a lighted room and office. A man sat behind a desk, watching Bart step from the elevator. The man was very tall and very thin, and the gray eyes, and the intensity of the lights, told Bart that he was a Mentorian. Raynor One?

Under the steady, stern gray stare, Bart felt the slow, clutching suck of fear again. Was this man a slave of the Lhari, who would turn him over to them? Or someone he could trust? His own mother had been a Mentorian.

"Who are you?" Raynor One's voice was harsh, and gave the impression of being loud, though it was not.

"David Briscoe."

It was the wrong thing. The Mentorian's mouth was taut, forbidding. "Try again. I happen to know that David Briscoe is dead."

"I have a message for Raynor Three."

The cold gray stare never altered. "On what business?"

On a sudden inspiration, Bart said, "I'll tell you that if you can tell me what the Eighth Color is."

There was a glint in the grim eyes now, though the even, stern voice did not soften. "I never knew myself. I didn't name it Eight Colors. Maybe it's the original owner you want."

On a sudden hope, Bart asked, "Was he, by any chance, named Rupert Steele?"

Raynor One made a suspicious movement. "I can't imagine why you think so," he said guardedly. "Especially if you've just come in from Earth. It was never very widely known. He only changed the name to Eight Colors a few weeks ago. And it's for sure that your ship didn't get any messages while the Lhari were in warp-drive. You mention entirely too many names, but I notice you aren't giving out any further information."

"I'm looking for a man called Rupert Steele."

"I thought you were looking for Raynor Three," said Raynor One, staring at the Mentorian cloak. "I can think of a lot of people who might want to know how I react to certain names, and find out if I know the wrong people, if they are the wrong people. What makes you think I'd admit it if I did?"

Now, Bart thought, they had reached a deadlock. Somebody had to trust somebody. This could go on all night—parry and riposte, question and evasive answer, each of them throwing back the other's questions in a verbal fencing-match. Raynor One wasn't giving away any information. And, considering what was probably at stake, Bart didn't blame him much.

He flung the Mentorian cloak down on the table.

"This got me out of trouble—the hard way," he said. "I never wore one before and I never intend to again. I want to find Rupert Steele because he's my father!"

"Your father. And just how are you going to prove that exceptionally interesting statement?"

Without warning, Bart lost his temper.

"I don't care whether I prove it or not! You try proving something for a change, why don't you? If you know Rupert Steele, I don't have to prove who I am—just take a good look at me! Or so Briscoe told me—a man who called himself Briscoe, anyway. He gave me papers to travel under that name! I didn't ask for them, he shoved them into my hand. That Briscoe is dead." Bart struck his fist hard on the desk, bending over Raynor One angrily.

"He sent me to find a man named Raynor Three. But the only one I really care about finding is my father. Now you know as much as I do, how about giving me some information for a change?"

He ran out of breath and stood glaring down at Raynor One, fists clenched. Raynor One got up and said, quick, savage and quiet, "Did anyone see you come here?"

"Only the girl downstairs."

"How did you get through the Lhari? In that?" He moved his head at the Mentorian cloak.

Bart explained briefly, and Raynor One shook his head.

"You were lucky," he said, "you could have been blinded. You must have inherited flash-accommodation from the Mentorian side—Rupert Steele didn't have it. I'll tell you this much," he added, sitting down again. "In a manner of speaking, you're my boss. Eight Colors—it used to be Alpha Transshipping—is what they call a middleman outfit. The interplanet cargo lines transport from planet to planet within a system—that's free competition—and the Lhari ships transport from star to star—that's a monopoly all over the galaxy. The middleman outfits arrange for orderly and businesslike liaison between the two. Rupert Steele bought into this company, a long time ago, but he left it for me to manage, until recently."

Raynor punched a button, said to the image of the glossy girl at the desk, "Violet, get Three for me. You may have to send a message to the Multiphase."

He swung round to Bart again. "You want a lot of explanations? Well, you'll have to get 'em from somebody else. I don't know what this is all about. I don't want to know: I have to do business with the Lhari. The less I know, the less I'm apt to say to the wrong people. But I promised Three that if you turned up, or if anyone came and asked for the Eighth Color, I'd send you to him. That's all."

He motioned Bart ungraciously to a seat, and shut his mouth firmly, as if he had already said too much. Bart sat. After a while he heard the elevator again; the panel slid open and Raynor Three came into the room.

It had to be Raynor Three; there was no one else he could have been. He was as like Raynor One as Tweedledum to Tweedledee: tall, stern, ascetic and grim. He wore the full uniform of a Mentorian on Lhari ships: the white smock of a medic, the metallic blue cloak, the low silvery sandals.

He said, "What's doing, One? Violet—" and then he caught sight of Bart. His eyes narrowed and he drew a quick breath, his face twisting up into apprehension and shock.

"It must be Steele's boy," he said, and immediately Bart saw the difference between the—were they brothers? For Raynor One's face, controlled and stern, had not altered all during their interview, but Raynor Three's smile was wry and kindly at once, and his voice was low and gentle. "He's the image of Rupert. Did he come in on his own name? How'd he manage it?"

"No. He had David Briscoe's papers."

"So the old man got through," said Raynor Three, with a low whistle. "But that's not safe. Quick, give them to me, Bart."

"The Lhari have them."

Raynor One walked to the window and said in his deadpan voice, "It's useless. But get the kid out of here before they come looking for me. Look."

He pointed. Below them, the streets were alive with uniformed Lhari and Mentorians. Bart felt sick.

"If they had the same efficiency with red tape that we humans have, he'd never have made it this far."

Raynor Three actually smiled. "But you can count on them for that much inefficiency," he said, and his eyes twinkled for a moment at Bart. "That's how it was so easy to work the old double-shuffle trick on them. They had Steele's description but not his name, so Briscoe took Steele's papers and managed to slip through. Once they landed on Earth, they had the Steele names, but by the time that cleared, you were outbound with another set of papers. It may have confused them, because they knew David Briscoe was dead—and there was just a chance you were an innocent bystander who could raise a real row if they pulled you in. Did old Briscoe get away?"

"No," Bart said, harshly, "he's dead."

Raynor Three's mobile face held shocked sadness. "Two brave men," he said softly, "Edmund Briscoe the father, David Briscoe the son. Remember the name, Bart, because I won't remember it."

"Why not?"

Raynor Three gave him a gold-glinting, enigmatic glance. "I'm a Mentorian, remember? I'm good at not remembering things. Just be glad I remember Rupert Steele. If you'd been a few days later, I wouldn't have remembered him, though I promised to wait for you."

Raynor One demanded, "Get him out of here, Three!"

Raynor Three swung to Bart. "Put that on again." He indicated the Mentorian cloak. "Pull the hood right up over your head. Now, if we meet anyone, say a polite good afternoon in Lhari—you can speak Lhari?—and leave the rest of the talking to me."

Bart felt like cringing as they came out into the street full of Lhari; but Raynor Three whispered, "Attack is the best defense," and went up to one of the Lhari. "What's going on, rieko mori?"

"A passenger on the ship got away without going through Decontam. He may spread disease, so of course we have alerted all authorities," the Lhari said.

As the Lhari strode past, Raynor Three grimaced. "Clever, that. Now the whole planet will be hunting for any stranger, worrying themselves into fits about some unauthorized germ. We'd better get you to a safe place. My country house is a good way off, but I have a copter."

Bart demanded, as they climbed in, "Are you taking me to my father?"

"Wait till we get to my place," Raynor Three said, taking the controls and putting the machine in the air. "Just lean back and enjoy the trip, huh?"

Bart relaxed against the cushions, but he still felt apprehensive. Where was his father? If he was a fugitive from the Lhari, he might by now be at the other end of the galaxy. But if his father couldn't travel on Lhari ships, and if he had been here, the chances were that he was still somewhere in the Procyon system.

They flew for a long time; across low hills, patchwork agricultural districts, towns, and then for a long time over water. The copter had automatic controls, but Raynor Three kept it on manual, and Bart wondered if the Mentorian just didn't want to talk.

It began to descend, at last, toward a small green hill, bright in the last gold rays on sunset. A small domelike pink bubble rose out of the hill. Raynor Three set the copter neatly down on a platform that slid shut after them, unfastened their seat belts and gave Bart a hand to climb out.

He ushered him into a living room of glass and chrome, softly lighted, but deserted and faintly dusty. Raynor pushed a switch; soft music came on, and the carpets caressed his feet. He motioned Bart to a chair.

"You're safe here, for a while," Raynor Three said, "though how long, nobody knows. But so far, I've been above suspicion.'"

Bart leaned back; the chair was very comfortable, but the comfort could not help him to relax.

"Where is my father?" he demanded.

Raynor Three stood looking down at him, his mobile face drawn and strange. "I guess I can't put it off any longer," he said softly. Then he covered his face with his hands. From behind them hoarse words came, choked with emotion.

"Your father is dead, Bart. I—I killed him."

Chapter Six

For a moment Bart stared, frozen, unable to move, his very ears refusing the words he heard. Had this all been another cruel trick, then, a trap, a betrayal? He rose and looked wildly around the room, as if the glass walls were a cage closing in on him.

"Murderer!" he flung at Raynor, and took a step toward him, his clenched fists coming up. He'd been shoved around too long, but here he had one of them right in front of him, and for once he'd hit back! He'd start by taking Raynor Three apart—in small pieces! "You—you rotten murderer!"

Raynor Three made no move to defend himself. "Bart," he said compassionately, "sit down and listen to me. No, I'm no murderer. I—I shouldn't have put it that way."

Bart's hands dropped to his sides, but he heard his voice crack with pain and grief: "I suppose you'll tell me he was a spy or a traitor and you had to kill him!"

"Not even that. I tried to save your father, I did everything I could. I'm no murderer, Bart. I killed him, yes—God forgive me, because I'll never forgive myself!"

Bart's fists unclenched and he stared down at Raynor Three, shaking his head in bewilderment and pain. "I knew he was dead! I knew it all along! I was trying not to believe it, but I knew!"

"I liked your father. I admired him. He took a long chance, and it killed him. I could have stopped him, I should have stopped him, but how could I? Where did I have the right to stop him, after what I did to—" he stopped, almost in mid-word, as if a switch had been turned.

But Bart was not listening. He swung away, striding to the wall as if he would kick it in, striking it with his two clenched fists, his whole being in revolt. Dad, oh, Dad! I kept going, I thought at the end of it you'd be here and it would all be over. But here I am at the end of it all, and you're not here, you won't ever be here again.

Dimly, he knew when Raynor Three rose and left him alone. He leaned his head on his clenched fists, and cried.

After a long time he raised his head and blew his nose, his face setting itself in new, hard, unaccustomed lines, slowly coming to terms with the hard, painful reality. His father was dead. His dangerous, dead-in-earnest game of escape had no happy ending of reunion with his father. They couldn't sit together and laugh about how scared he had been. His father was dead, and he, Bart, was alone and in danger. His face looked very grim indeed, and years older than he was.

After a long time Raynor Three opened the door quietly. "Come and have something to eat, Bart."

"I'm not hungry."

"Well, I am," Raynor Three said, "and you ought to be. You'll need it." He pulled knobs and the appropriate tables and chairs extruded themselves from the walls. Raynor unsealed hot cartons and spread them on the table, saying lightly, "Looks good—not that I can claim any credit, I subscribe to a food service that delivers them hot by pneumatic tube."

Bart felt sickened by the thought of eating, but when he put a polite fork in the food, he discovered that he was famished and ate up everything in sight. When they had finished, Raynor dumped the cartons into a disposal chute, went to a small portable bar and put a glass into his hand.

"Drink this."

Bart touched his lips to the glass, made a face and put it away. "Thanks, but I don't drink."

"Call it medicine, you'll need something," Raynor Three said crossly. "I've got a lot to tell you, and I don't want you going off half-primed in the middle of a sentence. If you'd rather have a shot of tranquilizer, all right; otherwise, I prescribe that you drink what I gave you." He gave Bart a quick, wry grin. "I really am a medic, you know."

Feeling like a scolded child, Bart drank. It burned his mouth, but after it was down, he felt a sort of warm burning in his insides that gradually spread a sense of well-being all through him. It wasn't alcohol, but whatever it was, it had quite a kick.

"Thanks," he muttered. "Why are you taking this trouble, Raynor? There must be danger—"

"Don't you know—" Raynor broke off. "Obviously, you don't. Your mother never said much about your Mentorian family tree, I suppose? She was a Raynor." He smiled at Bart, a little ruefully. "I won't claim a kinsman's privileges until you decide how much to trust me."

Raynor Three settled back.

"It's a long story and I only know part of it," he began. "Our family, the Raynors, have traded with the Lhari for more generations than I can count. When I was a young man, I qualified as a medic on the Lhari ships, and I've been star-hopping ever since. People call us the slaves of the Lhari—maybe we are," he added wryly. "But I began it just because space is where I belong, and there's nowhere else that I've ever wanted to be. And I'll take it at any price.

"I never questioned what I was doing until a few years ago. It was your father who made me wonder if we Mentorians were blind and selfish—this privilege ought to belong to everyone, not just the Lhari. More and more, the Lhari monopoly seemed wrong to me. But I was just a medic. And if I involved myself in any conspiracy against the Lhari, they'd find it out in the routine psych-checking.

"And then we worked out how it could be done. Before every trip, with self-hypnosis and self-suggestion, I erase my own memories—a sort of artificial amnesia—so that the Lhari can't find out any more than I want them to find out. Of course, it also means that I have no memory, while I'm on the Lhari ships, of what I've agreed to while I'm—" His face suddenly worked, and his mouth moved without words, as if he had run into some powerful barrier against speech.

It was a full minute, while Bart stared in dismay, before he found his voice again, saying, "So far, it was just a sort of loose network, trying to put together stray bits of information that the Lhari didn't think important enough to censor.

"And then came the big breakthrough. There was a young Apprentice astrogator named David Briscoe. He'd taken some runs in special test ships, and read some extremely obscure research data from the early days of the contact between men and Lhari, and he had a wild idea. He did the bravest thing anyone has ever done. He stripped himself of all identifying data—so that if he died, no one would be in trouble with the Lhari—and stowed away on a Lhari ship."

"But—" Bart's lips were dry—"didn't he die in the warp-drive?"

Slowly, Raynor Three shook his head.

"No, he didn't. No drugs, no cold-sleep—but he didn't die. Don't you see, Bart?" He leaned forward, urgently.

"It's all a fake! The Lhari have just been saying that to justify their refusal to give us the secret of the catalyst that generates the warp-drive frequencies! Such a simple lie, and it's worked for all these years!"

"A Mentorian found him and didn't have the heart to turn him over to the Lhari. So he was smuggled clear again. But when that Mentorian underwent the routine brain-checks at the end of the voyage, the Lhari found out what had happened. They didn't know Briscoe's name, but they wrung that Mentorian out like a wet dishcloth and got a description that was as good as fingerprints. They tracked down young Briscoe and killed him. They killed the first man he'd talked to. They killed the second. The third was your father."

"The murdering devils!"

Raynor sighed. "Your father and Briscoe's father were old friends. Briscoe's father was dying with incurable heart disease; his son was dead, and old Briscoe had only one thought in his mind—to make sure he didn't die for nothing. So he took your father's papers, knowing they were as good as a death warrant, slipped away and boarded a Lhari ship that led roundabout to stars where the message hadn't reached yet. He led them a good chase. Did he die or did they track him down and kill him?" Bart bowed his head and told the story.

"Meanwhile," Raynor Three continued, "your father came to me, knowing I was sympathetic, knowing I was a Lhari-trained surgeon. He had just one thought in his mind: to do, again, what David Briscoe had done, and make sure the news got out this time. He cooked up a plan that was even braver and more desperate. He decided to sign on a Lhari ship as a member of the crew."

"As a Mentorian?" Bart asked, but something cold, like ice water trickling down his back, told him this was not what Raynor meant. "The brainwashing—"

"No," said Raynor, "not as a Mentorian; he couldn't have escaped the psych-checking. As a Lhari."

Bart gasped. "How—"

"Men and Lhari are very much alike," Raynor Three said. "A few small things—skin color, the shape of the ears, the hands and claws—keep humans from seeing that the Lhari are men."

"Don't say that," Bart almost yelled. "Those filthy, murdering devils! You call those monsters men?"

"I've lived among the Lhari all my life. They're not devils, Bart, they have their reasons. Physiologically, the Lhari are—well, humanoid, if you like that better. They're a lot more like a man than a man is like, for instance, a gorilla. Your father convinced me that with minor plastic and facial surgery, he could pass as a Lhari. And finally I gave in, and did the surgery—"

"And it killed him!"

"Not really. It was a completely unforeseeable thing—a blood clot broke loose in a vein, and lodged in his brain. He was dead in seconds. It could have happened at any time," he said, "yet I feel responsible, even though I keep telling myself I'm not. And I'll help you as much as I can—for his sake, and for your mother's. The Lhari don't watch me too closely—they figure that anything I do they'll catch in the brainwashing. But I'm still one step ahead of them, as long as I can erase my own memories."

Bart was sifting it all, slowly, in his mind.

"Why was Dad doing this? What could he gain?"

"You know we can build ships as good as the Lhari ships, but we don't know anything about the rare catalyst they use for warp-drive fuel. Captain Steele had hopes of being able to discover where they got it."

"But couldn't they find out where the Lhari ships go for fueling?"

"No. There's no way to trail a Lhari ship," he reminded Bart. "We can follow them inside a star-system, but then they pop into warp-drive, and we don't know where they go when they aren't running between our stars.

"We've gathered together what information we do have, and we know that after a certain number of runs in our part of the galaxy, ships take off in the direction of Antares. There's a ship, due to come in here in about ten days, called the Swiftwing, which is just about due to make the Antares run. Captain Steele had managed to arrange—I don't know how, and I don't want to know how—for a vacancy on that ship, and somehow he got credentials. You see, it's a very good spy system, a network between the stars, but the weak link is this: everything, every message, every man, has to travel back and forth by the Lhari ships themselves."

He rose, shaking it all off impatiently. "Well, it's finished now. Your father is dead. What are you going to do? If you want to go back to Vega, you can probably convince the Lhari you're just an innocent bystander. They don't hurt bystanders or children, Bart. They aren't bad people. They're just protecting their business monopoly.

"The safest way to handle it would be this: let me erase your memories of what I've told you tonight. Then just let the Lhari capture you. They won't kill you. They'll just give you a light psych-check. When they find out you don't know anything, they'll send you back to Vega, and you can spend the rest of your life in peace, running Vega Interplanet and Eight Colors."

Bart turned on him furiously. "You mean, go home like a good little boy, and pretend none of this ever happened? What do you think I am, anyhow?"

Bart's chin set in the new, hard line. "What I want is a chance to go on where Dad left off!"

"It won't be easy, and it could be dangerous," Raynor Three said, "but there's nothing else to be done. We had the arrangements all made; and now somebody's got to take the dangerous risk of calling them off. Are you game for a little plastic surgery—just enough to change your looks again, with new forged papers? You can't go by the Swiftwing—it doesn't carry passengers—but there's another route you can take."

Bart sprang up. "No," he said, "I know a better way. Let me go on the Swiftwing—in Dad's place—as a Lhari!"

"Bart, no," Raynor Three said. "You'd never get away with it. It's too dangerous." But his gold eyes glinted.

"Why not? I speak Lhari better than Dad ever did. And my eyes can stand Lhari lights. You said yourself, it's going to be a dangerous job just calling off all the arrangements. So let's not call them off. Just let me take Dad's place!"

"Bart, you're only a boy—"

"What was Dave Briscoe? No, Raynor. Dad left me a lot more than Vega Interplanet, and you know it. I'll finish what he started, and then maybe I'll begin to deserve what he left me."

Raynor Three gripped Bart's hand. He said, in a voice that shook, "All right, Bart. You're your father's son. I can't say more than that. I haven't any right to stop you."

Chapter Seven

"All right, Bart, today we'll let you look at yourself," Raynor Three said.

Bart smiled under the muffling layers of bandage around his face. His hands were bandaged, too, and he had not been permitted to look in a mirror. But the transition had been surprisingly painless—or perhaps his sense of well-being had been due to Raynor Three slipping him some drug.

He'd been given injections of a chemical that would change the color of his skin; there had been minor operations on his face, his hands, his feet.

"Let's see you get up and walk around."

Bart obeyed awkwardly, and Raynor frowned. "Hurt?"

"Not exactly, but I feel as if I were limping."

"That's to be expected. I changed the angle of the heel tendon and the muscle of the arch. You're using a different set of muscles when you walk; until they harden up, you'll have some assorted Charley horses. Have any trouble hearing me?"

"No, though I'd hear better without all these bandages," Bart said impatiently.

"All in good time. Any trouble breathing?"

"No, except for the bandages."

"Fine. I changed the shape of your ears and nostrils, and it might have affected your hearing or your breathing. Now, listen, Bart: I'm going to take the bandages off your hands first. Sit down."

Bart sat across the table from him, obediently sticking out his hands. Raynor Three said, "Shut your eyes."

Bart did as he was told and felt Raynor Three's long fingers working at the bandages.

"Move each finger as I touch it." Bart obeyed, and Raynor said neutrally, "Good. Now, take a deep breath and then open your eyes."

Impatiently Bart flicked his lids open. In spite of the warning, his breath went out in a harsh, jolting gasp. His hands lay on the table before him—but they were not his hands.

The narrow, long fingers were pearl-gray, tipped with whitish-pink claws that curved out over the tips. Nervously Bart moved one finger, and the long claw flicked out like a cat's, retracted. He swallowed.

"Golly!" He felt strangely wobbly.

"A beautiful job, if I do say so. Be careful not to scratch yourself, and practice picking up small things."

Bart saw that the long grayish claws were trembling. "How did you make—the claws?"

"Quite simple, really," Raynor beamed. "I injected protein compounds into the nail matrix, which speeded up nail growth terrifically, and then, as they grew, shaped them. Joining on those tiny muscles for the retracting mechanism was the tricky part though."

Bart was moving his hands experimentally. Once over the shock, they felt quite normal. The claws didn't get in his way half so much as he'd expected when he picked up a pen that lay beside him and, with the blunt tip, made a few of the strange-looking dots and wedges that were the Lhari alphabet.

"Practice writing this," said Raynor Three, and laid a plastic-encased folder down beside him. It was a set of ship's papers printed in Lhari. Bart read it through, seeing that it was made out to the equivalent of Astrogator, First Class, Bartol.

"That's your name now, the name your father would have used. Memorize it, get used to the sound of it, practice writing it. Don't worry too much about the rating; it's an elementary one, what we'd call Apprentice rating, and I have a training tape for you anyhow. My brother got hold of it, don't ask me how—and don't ask him!"

"When am I going to see my face?"

"When I think you're ready for the shock," Raynor said bluntly. "It almost threw you when I showed you your hands."

He made Bart walk around some more briefly, slowly, he unwound the bandages; then turned and picked up a mirror at the bottom of his medic's case, turning it right side up. "Here. But take it easy."

But when Bart looked in the mirror he felt no unexpected shock, only an unnerving revulsion.

His hair was bleached-white and fluffy, almost feathery to the touch. His skin was grayish-rose, and his eyelids had been altered just enough to make his eyes look long, narrow and slanted. His nostrils were mere slits, and he moved his tongue over lips that felt oddly thin.

"I did as little to your teeth as I thought I could get away with-capped the front ones," Raynor Three told him. "So if you get a toothache you're out of luck—you won't dare go to a Lhari dentist. I could have done more, but it would have made you look too freakish when we changed you back to human again—if you live that long," he added grimly.

I hadn't thought about that. And if Raynor is going to forget me, who will do it? The cold knot of fear, never wholly absent, moved in him again.

Watching his face, Raynor Three said gently, "It's a big network, Bart. I'm not telling you much, for your own safety. But when you get to Antares, they'll tell you all you need to know."

He lifted Bart's oddly clawed hands. "I warned you, remember—the change isn't completely reversible. Your hands will always look—strange. The fingers had to be lengthened, for instance. I wanted to make you as safe as possible among the Lhari. I think you'll pass anything but an X-ray. Just be careful not to break any bones."

He gave Bart a package. "This is the Lhari training tape. Listen to it as often as you can, then destroy it—completely—before you leave here. The Swiftwing is due in port three days from now, and they stay here a week. I don't know how we'll manage it, but I'll guarantee there'll be a vacancy of one Astrogator, First Class, on that ship." He rose. "And now I'm going back to town and erase the memory." He stopped, looking intently at Bart.

"So if you see me, stay away from me and don't speak, because I won't know you from any other Lhari. Understand? From here on, you're on your own, Bart."

He held out his hand. "This is the rough part, Son." His face moved strangely. "I'm part of this network between the stars, but I don't know what I've done before, and I'll never know how it comes out. It's funny to stand here and look at you and realize that I won't even remember you." The gold-glinted eyes blinked rapidly. "Goodbye, Bart. And—good luck, Son."

Bart took his hand, deeply moved, with the strange sense that this was another death—a worse one than Briscoe's. He tried to speak and couldn't.

"Well—" Raynor's mouth twisted into a wry grin. "Ouch! Careful with those claws. The Lhari don't shake hands."

He turned abruptly and went out of the door and out of Bart's life, while Bart stood at the dome-window, feeling alone as he had never felt alone before.

He had to wait six days, and they felt like six eternities. He played the training tape over and over. With his Academy background, it wasn't nearly so difficult as he'd feared. He read and reread the set of papers identifying him as Astrogator, First Class, Bartol. Forged, he supposed. Or was there, somewhere, a real Bartol?

The last morning he slept uneasily late. He finished his last meal as a human, spent part of the day removing all traces of his presence from Raynor's home, burned the training tape, and finally got into the silky, silvery tights and cloak that Raynor had provided. He could use his hands now as if they belonged to him; he even found the claws handy and useful. He could write his signature, and copy out instructions from the training tape, without a moment's hesitation.

Toward dusk, a young Lhari slipped unobserved out of Raynor's house and hiked unnoticed to the edges of a small city nearby, where he mingled with the crowd and hired a skycab from an unobservant human driver to take him to the spaceport city. The skycab driver was startled, but not, Bart judged, unusually so, to pick up a Lhari passenger.

"Been doing a little sight-seeing on our planet, hey?"

"That's right," Bart said in Universal, not trying to fake his idea of the Lhari accent. Raynor had told him that only a few of the Lhari had that characteristic sibilant "r" and "s", and warned him against trying to imitate it. Just speak naturally; there are dialects of Lhari, just as there are dialects of the different human languages, and they all sound different in Universal anyhow. "Just looking around some."

The skycab driver frowned and looked down at his controls, and Bart felt curiously snubbed. Then he remembered. He himself had little to say to the Lhari when they spoke to him.

He was an alien, a monster. He couldn't expect to be treated like a human being any more.

When the skycab let him off before the spaceport, it felt strange to see how the crowds edged away from him as he made a way through them. He caught a glimpse of himself in one of the mirror-ramps, a tall thin strange form in a metallic cloak, head crested with feathery white, and felt overwhelmingly homesick for his own familiar face.

He was beginning to feel hungry, and realized that he could not go into an ordinary restaurant without attracting attention. There were refreshment stands all over the spaceport, and he briefly considered getting a snack at one of these.

No, that was just putting it off. The time had to come when he must face his fear and test his disguise among the Lhari themselves. Reviewing his knowledge of the construction of spaceports, he remembered that one side was the terminal, where humans and visitors and passengers were freely admitted; the other side, for Lhari and their Mentorian employees only, contained—along with business offices of many sorts—a sort of arcade with amusement centers, shops and restaurants catering to the personnel of the Lhari ships. With nine or ten ships docking every day, Raynor had assured him that a strange Lhari face would be lost in the crowds very easily.

He went to one of the doors marked danger, Lhari lights beyond, and passed through the glaring corridor of offices and storage-warehouses, finally coming out into a sort of wide mall. The lights were fierce, but he could endure them without trouble now, though his head ached faintly. Raynor, testing his light tolerance, had assured him that he could endure anything the Lhari could, without permanent damage to his optic nerves, though he would have headaches until he got used to them.

There were small shops and what looked like bars, and a glass-fronted place with a sign lettered largely, in black letters, a Lhari phrase meaning roughly home away from home: meals served, spacemen welcome, reasonable.

Behind him a voice said in Lhari, "Tell me, does that sign mean what it says? Or is this one of those traps for separating the unwary spaceman from his hard-earned credits? How's the food?"

Bart carefully took hold of himself.

"I was just wondering that myself." He turned as he spoke, finding himself face to face with a young Lhari in the unadorned cloak of a spaceman without official rank. He knew the Lhari was young because his crest was still white.

The young Lhari extended his claws in the closed-fist, hidden-claw gesture of Lhari greeting. "Shall we take a chance? Ringg son of Rahan greets you."

"Bartol son of Berihun."

"I don't remember seeing you in the port, Bartol."

"I've mostly worked on the Polaris run."

"Way off there?" Ringg son of Rahan sounded startled and impressed. "You really get around, don't you? Shall we sit here?"

They sat on triangular chairs at a three-cornered table. Bart waited for Ringg to order, and ordered what he did. When it came, it was a sort of egg-and-fish casserole which Bart found extremely tasty, and he dug into it with pleasure. Allowing for the claws, Lhari table manners were not so much different from human—and remember, their customs differ as much as ours do. If you do something differently, they'll just think you're from another planet with a different culture.

"Have you been here long?"

"A day or so. I'm off the Swiftwing."

Bart decided to hazard his luck. "I was told there's a vacancy on the Swiftwing."

Ringg looked at him curiously. "There is," he said, "but I'd like to know how you found it out. Captain Vorongil said that anyone who talked about it would be sent to Kleeto for three cycles. But what happened to you? Miss your ship?"

"No, I've just been laying off—traveling, sight-seeing, bumming around," Bart said. "But I'm tired of it, and now I'd like to sign out again."

"Well, we could use another man. This is the long run we're making, out to Antares and then home, and if everybody has to work extra shifts, it's no fun. But if old Vorongil knows that there's been talk in the port about Klanerol jumping ship, or whatever happened to him, we'll all have to walk wide of his temper."

Bart was beginning to relax a little; Ringg apparently accepted him without scrutiny. At this close range Ringg did not seem a monster, but just a young fellow like himself, hearty, good-natured—in fact, not unlike Tommy.

Bart chased the thought away as soon as it sneaked into his brain—one of those things, like Tommy? Then, rather grimly, he reminded himself, I'm one of those things. He said irritably, "So how do I account for asking your captain for the place?"

Ringg cocked his fluffy crest to one side. "I know," he said, "I told you. I'll say you're an old friend of mine. You don't know what Vorongil's like when he gets mad. But what he doesn't know, he won't shout about." He shoved back the triangular chair. "Who did tell you, anyway?"

This was the first real hurdle, and Bart's brain raced desperately, but Ringg was not listening for an answer. "I suppose somebody gossiped, or one of those fool Mentorians picked it up. Got your papers? What rating?"

"Astrogator first class."

"Klanerol was second, but you can't have everything, I suppose." Ringg led the way through the arcades, out across a guarded sector, passing half a dozen of the huge ships lying in their pits. Finally Ringg stopped and pointed. "This is the old hulk."

Bart had traveled only in Lhari passenger ships, which were new and fresh and sleek. This ship was enormous, ovoid like the egg of some space-monster, the sides dented and discolored, thin films of chemical discoloration lying over the glassy metallic hull.

Bart followed Ringg. This was real, it was happening. He was signing out for his first interstellar cruise on one of the Lhari ships. Not a Mentorian assistant, half-trusted, half-tolerated, but one of the crew themselves. If I'm lucky, he reminded himself grimly.

There was Lhari, in the black-banded officer's cloak, at the doorway. He glanced at Ringg's papers.

"Friend of mine," Ringg said, and Bart proffered his folder. The Lhari gave it a casual glance, handed it back.

"Old Baldy on board?" Ringg asked.

"Where else?" The officer laughed. "You don't think he'd relax with cargo not loaded, do you?"

They seemed casual and normal, and Bart's confidence was growing. They had accepted him as one of themselves. But the great ordeal still lay before him—an interview with the Lhari captain. And the idea had Bart sweating scared.

The corridors and decks seemed larger, wider, more spacious, but shabbier than on the clean, bright, commercial passenger decks Bart had seen. Dark-lensed men were rolling bales of cargo along on wheeled dollies. The corridors seemed endless. More to hear the sound of his own voice, and reassure himself of his ability to speak and be understood, than because he cared, he asked Ringg, "What's your rating?"

"Well, according to the logbooks, I'm an Expert Class Two, Metals-Fatigue," said Ringg. "That sounds very technical and interesting. But what it means is just that I go all over the ship inch by inch, and when I finish, start all over again at the other end. Most of what I do is just boss around the maintenance crews and snarl at them about spots of rust on the paint."

They got into a small round elevator and Ringg punched buttons; it began to rise, slowly and creakily, toward the top. "This, for instance," Ringg said. "I've been yelling for a new cable for six months." He turned. "Take it easy, Bartol; don't let Vorongil scare you. He likes to hear the sound of his own voice, but we'd all walk out the lock without spacesuits for him."

The elevator slid to a stop. The sign in Lhari letters said Level of Administration—Officers' Deck. Ringg pushed at a door and said, "Captain Vorongil?"

"I thought you were on leave," said a Lhari voice, deeper and slower than most. "What are you doing, back here more than ten milliseconds before strap-in checks?"

Ringg stepped back for Bart to go inside. The small cabin, with an elliptical bunk slung from the ceiling and a triangular table, was dwarfed by a tall, thin Lhari, in a cloak with four of the black bands that seemed to denote rank among them. He had a deeply lined face with a lacework of tiny wrinkles around the slanted eyes. His crest was not the high, fluffy white of a young

Lhari, but broken short near the scalp, grayish pink showing through, the little feathery ends yellowed with age. He growled, "Come in then, don't stand there. I suppose Ringg's told you what a tyrant I am? What do you want, feathertop?"

Bart remembered being told that this was the Lhari equivalent of "Kid" or "Youngster." He fumbled in the capacious folds of his cloak for his papers. His voice sounded shrill, even to himself.

"Bartol son of Berihun in respectful greeting, rieko mori." ("Honorable old-bald-one," the Lhari equivalent of "sir.") "Ringg told me there is a vacancy among the Astrogators, and I want to sign out."

Unmistakably, Vorongil's snort was laughter.

"So you've been talking, Ringg?"

Ringg retorted, "Better that I tell one man than that you have to hunt the planet over—or run the long haul with the drive-room watches short by one man."

"Well, well, you're right," Vorongil growled. He glared at Bart. "On the last planet, one of our men disappeared. Jumped ship!" The creases around his eyes deepened, troubled. "Probably just gone on the drift, sight-seeing, but I wish he'd told me. As it is, I wonder if he's been hurt, killed, kidnaped."

Ringg said, "Who'd dare? It would be reported."

Bart knew, with a cold chill, that the missing Klanerol had not simply gone "on the drift." No Lhari port would ever see Klanerol, Second Class Astrogator, again.

"Bartol," mused the captain, riffling the forged papers. "Served on the Polaris run. Hm—you are a good long way off your orbit, aren't you? Never been out that way myself. All right, I'll take you on. You can do system programming? Good. Rating in Second Galaxy mathematics?"

He nodded, hauled out a sheet of thin, wax-coated fabric and his claws made rapid imprints in the surface. He passed it to Bart, pointed. Bart hesitated, and Vorongil said impatiently, "Standard agreement, no hidden clauses. Put your mark on it, feathertop."

Bart realized it was something like a fingerprint they wanted. You'll pass anything but X-rays. He pressed the top of one claw into the wax. Vorongil nodded, shoved it on a shelf without looking at it.

"So much for that," said Ringg, laughing, as they came out. "The Bald One was in a good temper. I'm going to the port and celebrate, not that this dim place is very festive. You?"

"I—I think I'll stay aboard."

"Well, if you change your mind, I'll be down there somewhere," Ringg said. "See you later, shipmate." He raised his closed fist in farewell, and went.

Bart stood in the corridor, feeling astounded and strange. He belonged here! He had a right to be on board the ship! He wasn't quite sure what to do next.

A Lhari, as short and fat as a Lhari could possibly be and still be a Lhari, came or rather waddled out of the captain's office. He saw Bartol and called, "Are you the new First Class? I'm Rugel, coordinator."

Rugel had a huge cleft darkish scar across his lip, and there were two bands on his cloak. He was completely bald, and he puffed when he walked. "Vorongil asked me to show you around. You'll share quarters with Ringg—no sense shifting another man. Come down and see the chart rooms—or do you want to leave your kit in your cabin first?"

"I don't have much," Bart said.

Rugel's seamed lip widened. "That's the way—travel light when you're on the drift," he confirmed.

Rugel took him down to the drive rooms, and here for a moment, in wonder and awe, Bart almost forgot his disguise. The old Lhari led him to the huge computer which filled one wall of the room, and Bart was smitten with the universality of mathematics. Here was something he knew he could handle.

He could do this programming, easily enough. But as he stood before the banks of complex, yet beautifully familiar levers, the sheer exquisite complexity of it overcame him. To compute the movements of thousands of stars, all moving at different speeds in different directions in the vast swirling directionless chaos of the Universe—and yet to be sure that every separate movement would come out to within a quarter of a mile! It was something that no finite brain—man or Lhari—could ever accomplish, yet their limited brains had built these computers that could do it.

Rugel watched him, laughing softly. "Well, you'll have enough time down here. I like to have youngsters who are still in the middle of a love affair with their work. Come along, and I'll show you your cabin."

Rugel left him in a cabin amidships; small and cramped, but tidy, two of the oval bunks slung at opposite ends, a small table between them, and drawers filled with pamphlets and manuals and maps. Furtively, ashamed of himself, yet driven by necessity, Bart searched Ringg's belongings, wanting to get some idea of what possessions he ought to own. He looked around the shower and toilet facilities with extra care—this was something he couldn't slip up on and be considered even halfway normal. He was afraid Ringg would come in, and see him staring curiously at something as ordinary, to a Lhari, as a cake of soap.

He decided to go down to the port again and look around the shops. He was not afraid of being unable to handle his work. What he feared was something subtler—that the small items of everyday living, something as simple as a nail file, would betray him.

On his way he looked into the Recreation Lounge, filled with comfortable seats, vision-screens, and what looked like simple pinball machines and mechanical games of skill. There were also stacks of tapereels and headsets for listening, not unlike those humans used. Bart felt fascinated, and wanted to explore, but decided he could do that later.

Somehow he took the wrong turn coming out of the Recreation Lounge, and went through a door where the sudden dimming of lights told him he was in Mentorian quarters. The sudden darkness made him stumble, thrust out his hands to keep from falling, and an unmistakably human voice said, "Ouch!"

"I'm sorry," Bart said in Universal, without thinking.

"I admit the lights are dim," said the voice tartly, and Bart found himself looking down, as his eyes adjusted to the new light level, at a girl.

She was small and slight, in a metallic blue cloak that swept out, like wings, around her thin shoulders; the hood framed a small, kittenlike face. She was a Mentorian, and she was human, and Bart's eyes rested with comfort on her face; she, on the other hand, was looking up with anxiety and uneasy distrust. That's right—I'm a Lhari, a nonhuman freak!

"I seem to have missed my way."

"What are you looking for, sir? The medical quarters are through here."

"I'm looking for the elevator down to the crew exits."

"Through here," she said, reopening the door through which he had come, and shading her large, lovely, long-lashed eyes with a slender hand. "You took the wrong turn. Are you new on board? I thought all ships were laid out exactly alike."

"I've only worked on passenger ships."

"I believe they are somewhat different," said the girl in good Lhari. "Well, that is your way, sir."

He felt as if he had been snubbed and dismissed.

"What is your name?"

She stiffened as if about to salute. "Meta of the house of Marnay Three, sir."

Bart realized he was doing something wholly out of character for a Lhari—chatting casually with a Mentorian. With a wistful glance at the pretty girl, he said a stiff "Thank you" and went down the ramp she had indicated. He felt horribly lonely. Being a freak wasn't going to be much fun.

Chapter Eight

He saw the girl again next day, when they checked in for blastoff. She was seated at a small desk, triangular like so much of the Lhari furniture, checking a register as they came out of the Decontam room, making sure they downed their greenish solution of microorganisms.

"Papers, please?" She marked, and Bart noticed that she was using a red pencil.

"Bartol," she said aloud. "Is that how you pronounce it?" She made small scribbles in a sort of shorthand with the red pencil, then made other marks with the black one in Lhari; he supposed the red marks were her own private memoranda, unreadable by the Lhari.

"Next, please." She handed a cup of the greenish stuff to Ringg, behind him. Bart went down toward the drive room, and to his own surprise, found himself wishing the girl were a mathematician rather than a medic. It would have been pleasant to watch her down there.

Old Rugel, on duty in the drive room, watched Bart strap himself in before the computer. "Make sure you check all dials at null," he reminded him, and Bart felt a last surge of panic.

This was his first cruise, except for practice runs at the Academy! Yet his rating called him an experienced man on the Polaris run. He'd had the Lhari training tape, which was supposed to condition his responses, but would it? He tried to clench his fists, drove a claw into his palm, winced, and commanded himself to stay calm and keep his mind on what he was doing.

It calmed him to make the routine check of his dials.

"Strapdown check," said a Lhari with a yellowed crest and a rasping voice. "New man, eh?" He gave Bart's straps perfunctory tugs at shoulders and waist, tightened a buckle. "Karol son of Garin."

Bells rang in the ship, and Bart felt the odd, tonic touch of fear. This was it.

Vorongil strode through the door, his banded cloak sweeping behind him, and took the control couch.

"Ready from fueling room, sir."

"Position," Vorongil snapped.

Bart heard himself reading off a string of figures in Lhari. His voice sounded perfectly calm.

"Communication."

"Clear channels from Pylon Dispatch, sir." It was old Rugel's voice.

"Well," Vorongil said, slowly and almost reflectively, "let's take her up then."

He touched some controls. The humming grew. Then, swift, hard and crushing, weight mashed Bart against his couch.

"Position!" Vorongil's voice sounded harsh, and Bart fought the crushing weight of it. Even his eyeballs ached as he struggled to turn the tiny eye muscles from dial to dial, and his voice was a dim croak: "Fourteen seven sidereal twelve point one one four nine...."

"Hold it to point one one four six," Vorongil said calmly.

"Point one one four six," Bart said, and his claws stabbed at dials. Suddenly, in spite of the cold weight on his chest, the pain, the struggle, he felt as if he were floating. He managed a long, luxurious breath. He could handle it. He knew what he was doing.

He was an Astrogator....

Later, when Acceleration One had reached its apex and the artificial gravity made the ship a place of comfort again, he went down to the dining hall with Ringg and met the crew of the Swiftwing. There were twelve officers and twelve crewmen of various ratings like himself and Ringg, but there seemed to be little social division between them, as there would have been on a human ship; officers and crew joked and argued without formality of any kind.

None of them gave him a second look. Later, in the Recreation Lounge, Ringg challenged him to a game with one of the pinball machines. It seemed fairly simple to Bart; he tried it, and to his own surprise, won.

Old Rugel touched a lever at the side of the room. With a tiny whishing sound, shutters opened, the light of Procyon Alpha flooded them and he looked out through a great viewport into bottomless space.

Procyon Alpha, Beta and Gamma hung at full, rings gently tilted. Beyond them the stars burned, flaming through the shimmers of cosmic dust. The colors, the never-ending colors of space!

And he stood here, in a room full of monsters—he was one of the monsters—

"Which one of the planets was it we stopped on?" Rugel asked. "I can't tell 'em apart from this distance."

Bartol swallowed; he had almost said the blue one. He pointed. "The—the big one there, with the rings almost edge-on. I think they call it Alpha."

"It's their planet," said Rugel. "I guess they can call it what they want to. How about another game?"

Resolutely, Bart turned his back on the bewitching colors, and bent over the pinball machine.

The first week in space was a nightmare of strain. He welcomed the hours on watch in the drive room; there alone he was sure of what he was doing. Everywhere else in the ship he was perpetually scared, perpetually on tiptoe, perpetually afraid of making some small and stupid mistake. Once he actually called Aldebaran a red star, but Rugel either did not hear the slip or thought he was repeating what one of the Mentorians—there were two aboard besides the girl—had said.

The absence of color from speech and life was the hardest thing to get used to. Every star in the manual was listed by light-frequency waves, to be checked against a photometer for a specific reading, and it almost drove Bart mad to go through the ritual when the Mentorians were off duty and could not call off the color and the equivalent frequency type for him. Yet he did not dare skip a single step, or someone might have guessed that he could see the difference between a yellow and a green star before checking them.

The Academy ships had had the traditional human signal system of flashing red lights. Bart was stretched taut all the time, listening for the small codelike buzzers and ticks that warned him of filled tanks, leads in need of servicing, answers ready. Ringg's metal-fatigues testing kit was a bewildering muddle of boxes, meters, rods and earphones, each buzzing and clicking its characteristic warning.

At first he felt stretched to capacity every waking moment, his memory aching with a million details, and lay awake nights thinking his mind would crack under the strain. Then Alpha faded to a dim bluish shimmer, Beta was eclipsed, Gamma was gone, Procyon dimmed to a failing spark; and suddenly Bart's memory accustomed itself to the load, the new habits were firmly in place, and he found himself eating, sleeping and working in a settled routine.

He belonged to the Swiftwing now.

Procyon was almost lost in the viewports when a sort of upswept tempo began to run through the ship, an undercurrent of increased activity. Cargo was checked, inventoried and strapped in. Ringg was given four extra men to help him, made an extra tour of the ship, and came back buzzing like a frantic cricket. Bart's computers told him they were forging toward the sidereal location assigned for the first of the warp-drive shifts, which would take them some fifteen light-years toward Aldebaran.

On the final watch before the warp-drive shift, the medical officer came around and relieved the Mentorians from duty. Bart watched them go, with a curious, cold, crawling apprehension. Even the Mentorians, trusted by the Lhari—even these were put into cold-sleep! Fear grabbed his insides.

No human had ever survived the shift into warp-drive, the Lhari said. Briscoe, his father, Raynor Three—they thought they had proved that the Lhari lied. If they were right, if it was a Lhari trick to reinforce their stranglehold on the human worlds and keep the warp-drive for themselves, then Bart had nothing to fear. But he was afraid.

Why did the Mentorians endure this, never quite trusted, isolated among aliens?

Raynor Three had said, Because I belong in space, because I'm never happy anywhere else. Bart looked out the viewport at the swirl and burn of the colors there. Now that he could never speak of the colors, it seemed he had never been so wholly and wistfully aware of them. They symbolized the thing he could never put into words.

So that everyone can have this. Not just the Lhari.

Rugel watched the Mentorians go, scowling. "I wish medic would find a way to keep them alive through warp," he said. "My Mentorian assistant could watch that frequency-shift as we got near the bottom of the arc, and I'll bet she could see it. They can see the changes in intensity faster than I can plot them on the photometer!"

Bart felt goosebumps break out on his skin. Rugel spoke as if the certain death of humans, Mentorians, was a fact. Didn't the Lhari themselves know it was a farce? Or was it?

Vorongil himself took the controls for the surge of Acceleration Two, which would take them past the Light Barrier. Bart, watching his instruments to exact position and time, saw the colors of each star shift strangely, moment by moment. The red stars seemed hard to see. The orange-yellow ones burned suddenly like flame; the green ones seemed golden, the blue ones almost green. Dimly, he remembered the old story of a "red shift" in the lights of approaching stars, but here he saw it pure, a sight no human eyes had ever seen. A sight that no eyes had seen, human or otherwise, for the Lhari could not see it....

"Time," he said briefly to Vorongil, "Fifteen seconds...."

Rugel looked across from his couch. Bart felt that the old, scarred Lhari could read his fear. Rugel said through a wheeze, "No matter how old you get,

Bartol, you're still scared when you make a warp-shift. But relax, computers don't make mistakes."

"Catalyst," Vorongil snapped, "Ready—shift!"

At first there was no change; then Bart realized that the stars, through the viewport, had altered abruptly in size and shade and color. They were not sparks but strange streaks, like comets, crossing and recrossing long tails that grew, longer and longer, moment by moment. The dark night of space was filled with a crisscrossing blaze. They were moving faster than light, they saw the light left by the moving Universe as each star hurled in its own invisible orbit, while they tore incredibly through it, faster than light itself....

Bart felt a curious, tingling discomfort, deep in his flesh; almost an itching, a stinging in his very bones.

Lhari flesh is no different from ours....

Space, through the viewport, was no longer space as he had come to know it, but a strange eerie limbo, the star-tracks lengthening, shifting color until they filled the whole viewport with shimmering, gray, recrossing light. The unbelievable reaction of warp-drive thrust them through space faster than the lights of the surrounding stars, faster than imagination could follow.

The lights in the drive chamber began to dim—or was he blacking out? The stinging in his flesh was a clawed pain.

Briscoe lived through it....

They say.

The whirling star-tracks fogged, coiled, turned colorless worms of light, went into a single vast blur. Dimly Bart saw old Rugel slump forward, moaning softly; saw the old Lhari pillow his bald head on his veined arms. Then darkness took him; and thinking it was death, Bart felt only numb, regretful failure. I've failed, we'll always fail. The Lhari were right all long.

But we tried! By God, we tried!

"Bartol?" A gentle hand, cat claws retracted, came down on his shoulder. Ringg bent over him. Good-natured rebuke was in his voice. "Why didn't you tell us you got a bad reaction, and ask to sign out for this shift?" he demanded. "Look, poor old Rugel's passed out again. He just won't admit he can't take it—but one idiot on a watch is enough! Some people just feel as if the bottom's dropped out of the ship, and that's all there is to it."

Bart hauled his head upright, fighting a surge of stinging nausea. His bones itched inside and he was damnably uncomfortable, but he was alive.

"I'm—fine."

"You look it," Ringg said in derision. "Think you can help me get Rugel to his cabin?"

Bart struggled to his feet, and found that when he was upright he felt better. "Wow!" he muttered, then clamped his mouth shut. He was supposed to be an experienced man, a Lhari hardened to space. He said woozily, "How long was I out?"

"The usual time," Ringg said briskly, "about three seconds—just while we hit peak warp-drive. Feels longer, so they tell me, sometimes—time's funny, beyond light-speeds. The medic says it's purely psychological. I'm not so sure. I itch, blast it!"

He moved his shoulders in a squirming way, then bent over Rugel, who was moaning, half insensible. "Catch hold of his feet, Bartol. Here—ease him out of his chair. No sense bothering the medics this time. Think you can manage to help me carry him down to the deck?"

"Sure," Bart said, finding his feet and his voice. He felt better as they moved along the hallway, the limp, muttering form of the old Lhari insensible in their arms. They reached the officer's deck, got Rugel into his cabin and into his bunk, hauled off his cloak and boots. Ringg stood shaking his head.

"And they say Captain Vorongil's so tough!"

Bart made a questioning noise.

"Why, just look," said Ringg. "He knows it would make poor old Rugel feel as if he wasn't good for much—to order him into his bunk and make him take dope like a Mentorian for every warp-shift. So we have this to go through at every jump!" He sounded cross and disgusted, but there was a rough, boyish gentleness as he hauled the blanket over the bald old Lhari. He looked up, almost shyly.

"Thanks for helping me with Old Baldy. We usually try to get him out before Vorongil officially takes notice. Of course, he sort of keeps his back turned," Ringg said, and they laughed together as they turned back to the drive room. Bart found himself thinking, Ringg's a good kid, before he pulled himself up, in sudden shock.

He had lived through warp-drive! Then, indeed, the Lhari had been lying all along, the vicious lie that maintained their stranglehold monopoly of star-travel. He was their enemy again, the spy within their gates, like Briscoe, to be hunted down and killed, but to bring the message, loud and clear, to everyone: The Lhari lied! The stars can belong to us all!

When he got back to the drive room, he saw through the viewport that the blur had vanished, the star-trails were clear, distinct again, their comet-tails shortening by the moment, their colors more distinct.

The Lhari were waiting, a few poised over their instruments, a few more standing at the quartz window watching the star-trails, some squirming and scratching and grousing about "space fleas"—the characteristic itching reaction that seemed to be deep down inside the bones.

Bart checked his panels, noted the time when they were due to snap back into normal space, and went to stand by the viewport. The stars were reappearing, seeming to steady and blaze out in cloudy splendor through the bright dust. They burned in great streamers of flame, and for the moment he forgot his mission again, lost in the beauty of the fiery lights. He drew a deep, shaking gasp. It was worth it all, to see this! He turned and saw Ringg, silent, at his shoulder.

"Me, too," Ringg said, almost in a whisper. "I think every man on board feels that way, a little, only he won't admit it." His slanted gray eyes looked quickly at Bart and away.

"I guess we're almost down to L-point. Better check the panel and report nulls, so medic can wake up the Mentorians."

The Swiftwing moved on between the stars. Aldebaran loomed, then faded in the viewports; another shift jumped them to a star whose human name Bart did not know. Shift followed shift, spaceport followed spaceport, sun followed sun; men lived on most of these worlds, and on each of them a Lhari spaceport rose, alien and arrogant. And on each world men looked at Lhari with resentful eyes, cursing the race who kept the stars for their own.

Cargo amassed in the holds of the Swiftwing, from worlds beyond all dreams of strangeness. Bart grew, not bored, but hardened to the incredible. For days at a time, no word of human speech crossed his mind.

The blackout at peak of each warp-shift persisted. Vorongil had given him permission to report off duty, but since the blackouts did not impair his efficiency, Bart had refused. Rugel told him that this was the moment of equilibrium, the peak of the faster-than-light motion.

"Perhaps a true limiting speed beyond which nothing will ever go," Vorongil said, touching the charts with a varnished claw. Rugel's scarred old mouth spread in a thin smile.

"Maybe there's no such thing as a limiting speed. Someday we'll reach true simultaneity—enter warp, and come out just where we want to be, at the same time. Just a split-second interval. That will be real transmission."

Ringg scoffed, "And suppose you get even better—and come out of warp before you go into it? What then, Honorable Bald One?"

Rugel chuckled, and did not answer. Bart turned away. It was not easy to keep on hating the Lhari.

There came a day when he came on watch to see drawn, worried faces; and when Ringg came into the drive room they threw their levers on automatic and crowded around him, their crests bobbing in question and dismay. Vorongil seemed to emit sparks as he barked at Ringg, "You found it?"

"I found it. Inside the hull lining."

Vorongil swore, and Ringg held up a hand in protest. "I only locate metals fatigue, sir—I don't make it!"

"No help for it then," Vorongil said. "We'll have to put down for repairs. How much time do we have, Ringg?"

"I give it thirty hours," Ringg said briefly, and Vorongil gave a long shrill whistle. "Bartol, what's the closest listed spaceport?"

Bart dived for handbooks, manuals, comparative tables of position, and started programming information. The crew drifted toward him, and by the time he finished feeding in the coded information, a row three-deep of Lhari surrounded him, including all the officers. Vorongil was right at his shoulder when Bart slipped on his earphones and started decoding the punched strips that fed out the answers from the computer.

"Nearest port is Cottman Four. It's almost exactly thirty hours away."

"I don't like to run it that close." Vorongil's face was bitten deep with lines. He turned to Ramillis, head of Maintenance. "Do we need spare parts? Or just general repairs?"

"Just repairs, sir. We have plenty of shielding metal. It's a long job to get through the hulls, but there's nothing we can't fix."

Vorongil flexed his clawed hands nervously, stretching and retracting them. "Ringg, you're the fatigue expert. I'll take your word for it. Can we make thirty hours?"

Ringg looked pale and there was none of his usual boyish nonsense when he said, "Captain, I swear I wouldn't risk Cottman. You know what crystallization's like, sir. We can't get through that hull lining to repair it in space, if it does go before we land. We wouldn't have the chance of a hydrogen atom in a tank of halogens."

Vorongil's slanted eyebrows made a single unbroken line. "That's the word then. Bartol, find us the closest star with a planet—spaceport or not."

Bart's hands were shaking with sudden fear. He checked each digit of their present position, fed it into the computer, waited, finally wet his lips and plunged, taking the strip from a computer.

"This small star, called Meristem. It's a—" he bit his lip, hard; he had almost said green—"type Q, two planets with atmosphere within tolerable limits, not classified as inhabited."

"Who owns it?"

"I don't have that information on the banks, sir."

Vorongil beckoned the Mentorian assistant. So apart were Lhari and Mentorian on these ships that Bart did not even know his name. He said, "Look up a star called Meristem for us." The Mentorian hurried away, came back after a moment with the information that it belonged to the Second Galaxy Federation, but was listed as unexplored.

Vorongil scowled. "Well, we can claim necessity," he said. "It's only eight hours away, and Cottman's thirty. Bartol, plot us a warp-drive shift that will land us in that system, and on the inner of the two planets, within nine hours. If it's a type Q star, that means dim illumination, and no spaceport mercury-vapor installations. We'll need as much sunlight as we can get."

It was the first time that Bart, unaided, had had the responsibility of plotting a warp-drive shift. He checked the coordinates of the small green star three times before passing them along to Vorongil. Even so, when they went into Acceleration Two, he felt stinging fear. *If I plotted wrong, we could shift into that crazy space and come out billions of miles away....*

But when the stars steadied and took on their own colors, the blaze of a small green sun was steady in the viewport.

"Meristem," Vorongil said, taking the controls himself. "Let's hope the place is really uninhabited and that catalogue's up to date, lads. It wouldn't be any fun to burn up some harmless village, or get shot at by barbarians—and we're setting down with no control-tower signals and no spaceport repair crews. So let's hope our luck holds out for a while yet."

Bart, feeling the minute, unsteady trembling somewhere in the ship—*Imagination*, he told himself, *you can't feel metal-fatigue somewhere in the hull lining*—echoed the wish. He did not know that he had already had the best luck of his unique voyage, or realize the fantastic luck that had brought him to the small green star Meristem.

Chapter Nine

The crews of repairmen were working down in the hull, and the Swiftwing was a hell of clanging noise and shuddering heat. Maintenance was working overtime, but the rest of the crew, with nothing to do, stood around in the recreation rooms, tried to play games, cursed the heat and the dreary dimness through the viewports, and twitched at the boiler-factory racket from the holds.

Toward the end of the third day, the biologist reported air, water and gravity well within tolerable limits, and Captain Vorongil issued permission for anyone who liked, to go outside and have a look around.

Bart had a sort of ship-induced claustrophobia. It was good to feel solid ground under his feet and the rays of a sun, even a green sun, on his back. Even more, it was good to get away from the constant presence of his shipmates. During this enforced idleness, their presence oppressed him unendurably—so many tall forms, gray skins, feathery crests. He was always alone; for a change, he felt that he'd like to be alone without Lhari all around him.

But as he moved away from the ship, Ringg dropped out of the hatchway and hailed him. "Where are you going?"

"Just for a walk."

Ringg drew a deep breath of weariness. "That sounds good. Mind if I come along?"

Bart did, but all he could say was, "If you like."

"How about let's get some food from the rations clerk, and do some exploring?"

The sun overhead was a clear greenish-gold, the sky strewn with soft pale clouds that cast racing shadows on the soft grass underfoot, fragrant pinkish-yellow stuff strewn with bright vermilion puff-balls. Bart wished he were alone to enjoy it.

"How are the repairs coming?"

"Pretty well. But Karol got his hand half scorched off, poor fellow. Just luck the same thing didn't happen to me." Ringg added. "You know that Mentorian—the young one, the medic's assistant?"

"I've seen her. Her name's Meta, I think." Suddenly, Bart wished the Mentorian girl were with him here. It would be nice to hear a human voice.

"Oh, is it a female? Mentorians all look alike to me," Ringg said, while Bart controlled his face with an effort. "Be that as it may, she saved me from having the same thing happen. I was just going to lean against a strip of sheet metal when she screamed at me. Do you think they can really see heat vibrations? She called it red-hot."

They had reached a line of tall cliffs, where a steep rock-fall divided off the plain from the edge of the mountains. A few slender, drooping, gold-leaved trees bent graceful branches over a pool. Bart stood fascinated by the play of green sunlight on the emerald ripples, but Ringg flung himself down full length on the soft grass and sighed comfortably. "Feels good."

"Too comfortable to eat?"

They munched in companionable silence. "Look," said Ringg at last, pointing toward the cliffs, "Holes in the rocks. Caves. I'd like to explore them, wouldn't you?"

"They look pretty gloomy to me. Probably full of monsters."

Ringg patted the hilt of his energon-ray. "This will handle anything short of an armor-plated saurian."

Bart shuddered. As part of uniform, he, too, had been issued one of the energon-rays; but he had never used it and didn't intend to. "Just the same, I'd rather stay out here in the sun."

"It's better than vitamin lamps," Ringg admitted, "even if it's not very bright."

Bart wondered, suddenly and worriedly, about the effects of green sunburn on his chemically altered skin tone.

"Well, let's enjoy it while we can," Ringg said, "because it seems to be clouding over. I wouldn't be surprised if it rained." He yawned. "I'm getting bored with this voyage. And yet I don't want it to end, because then I'll have to fight it out all over again with my family. My father owns a hotel, and he wants me in the family business, not five hundred light-years away. None of our family have ever been spacemen before," he explained, "and they don't understand that living on one planet would drive me out of my mind." He sighed. "How did you explain it to your people—that you couldn't be happy in the mud? Or are you a career man?"

"I guess so. I never thought about doing anything else," Bart said slowly, Ringg's story had touched him; he had never realized quite so fully how much alike the two races were, how human the Lhari problems and dreams could seem. Why, of course, the Lhari aren't all spacemen. They have hotel keepers and garbage men and dentists just as we do. Funny, you never think of them except in space.

"My mother died when I was very young," Bart said, choosing his words very carefully. "My father owned a fleet of interplanetary ships."

"But you wanted the real thing, deep space, the stars," Ringg said. "How did he feel about that?"

"He would have understood," Bart said, unable to keep emotion out of his voice, "but he's dead now. He died, not long ago."

Ringg's eyes were bright with sympathy. "While you were off on the drift? Bad luck," he said gently. He was silent, and when he spoke again it was in a very different tone.

"But some of the older generation—I had a professor in training school, funny old chap, bald as the hull of the Swiftwing. Taught us cosmic-ray analysis, and what he didn't know about spiral nebulae could be engraved on my fifth toe-claw, and he'd never been off the face of the planet. Not even to one of the moons! He was the supervisor of my student lodge, and oh, was he a—" The phrase Ringg used meant, literally, a soft piece of cake.

"His feet may have been buried in mud, but his head was off in the Great Nebula. We had some wild times," Ringg reminisced. "We'd slip away to the city—strictly against rules, it was an old-style school—and draw lots for one of us to stay home and sign in for all twelve. You see, he'd sit there reading, and when one of us came in, just shove the wax at us, with his nose in a text on cosmic dust, never looking up. So the one who stayed home would scrawl a name on it, walk out the back door, come around and sign in again. When there were twelve signed in, of course, the old chap would go up to bed, and late that night the one who stayed in would sneak down and let us in."

Ringg sat up suddenly, touching his cheek. "Was that a drop of rain? And the sun's gone. I suppose we ought to start back, though I hate to leave those caves unexplored."

Bart bent to gather up the debris of their meal. He flinched as something hard struck his arm. "Ouch! What was that?"

Ringg cried out in pain. "It's hail!"

Sharp pieces of ice were suddenly pelting, raining down all around them, splattering the ground with a harsh, bouncing clatter. Ringg yelled, "Come on—it's big enough to flatten you!"

It looked to Bart as if it were at least golf-ball size, and seemed to be getting bigger by the moment. Lightning flashed around them in sudden glare. They ducked their heads and ran.

"Get in under the lee of the cliffs. We couldn't possibly make it back to the Swift—" Ringg's voice broke off in a cry of pain; he slumped forward, pitched to his knees, then slid down and lay still.

"What's the matter?" Bart, arm curved to protect his skull, bent over the fallen Lhari, but Ringg, his forehead bleeding, lay insensible. Bart felt sharp pain in his arm, felt the hail hard as thrown stones raining on his head. Ringg was out cold. If they stayed in this, Bart thought despairingly, they'd both be dead!

Crouching, trying to duck his head between his shoulders, Bart got his arms under Ringg's armpits and half-carried, half-dragged him under the lee of the cliffs. He slipped and slid on the thickening layer of ice underfoot, lost his footing, and came down, hard, one arm twisted between himself and the cliff. He cried out in pain, uncontrollably, and let Ringg slip from his grasp. The Lhari boy lay like the dead.

Bart bent over him, breathing hard, trying to get his breath back. The hail was still pelting down, showing no signs of lessening. About five feet away, one of the dark gaps in the cliff showed wide and menacing, but at least, Bart thought, the hail couldn't come in there. He stooped and got hold of Ringg again. A pain like fire went through the wrist he had smashed against the rock. He set his teeth, wondering if it had broken. The effort made him see stars, but he managed somehow to hoist Ringg up again and haul him through the pelting hail toward the yawning gap. It darkened around them, and, blessedly, the battering, bruising hail could not reach them. Only an occasional light splinter of ice blew with the bitter wind into the mouth of the cave.

Bart laid Ringg down on the floor, under the shelter of the rock ceiling. He knelt beside him, and spoke his name, but Ringg just moaned. His forehead was covered with blood.

Bart took one of the paper napkins from the lunch sack and carefully wiped some of it away. His stomach turned at the deep, ugly cut, which immediately started oozing fresh blood. He pressed the edges of the cut together with the napkin, wondering helplessly how much blood Ringg could lose without danger, and if he had concussion. If he tried to go back to the ship and fetch the medic for Ringg, he'd be struck by hail himself. From where he stood, it seemed that the hailstones were getting bigger by the minute.

Ringg moaned, but when Bart knelt beside him again he did not answer. Bart could hear only the rushing of wind, the noise of the splattering hail and a sound of water somewhere—or was that a rustle of scales, a dragging of strange feet? He looked through the darkness into the depths of the cave, his hand on his shock-beam. He was afraid to turn his back on it.

This is nonsense, he told himself firmly, I'll just walk back there and see what there is.

At his belt he had the small flashlamp, excessively bright, that was, like the energon-beam shocker, a part of regulation equipment. He took it out, shining it on the back wall of the cave; then drew a long breath of startlement and for a moment forgot Ringg and his own pain.

For the back wall of the cave was an exquisite fall of crystal! Minerals glowed there, giant crystals, like jewels, crusted with strange lichen-like growths and colors. There were pale blues and greens and, shimmering among them, a strangely colored crystalline mineral that he had never seen before. It was blue—No, Bart thought, that's just the light, it's more like red—no, it can't be like both of them at once, and it isn't really like either. In this light—

Ringg moaned, and Bart, glancing round, saw that he was struggling to sit up. He ran back to him, dropping to his knees at Ringg's side. "It's all right, Ringg, lie still. We're under cover now."

"Wha' happened?" Ringg said blurrily. "Head hurts—all sparks—all the pretty lights—can't see you!" He fumbled with loose, uncoordinated fingers at his head and Bart grabbed at him before he poked a claw in his eye. "Don't do that," Ringg complained, "can't see—"

He must have a bad concussion then. That's a nasty cut. Gently, he restrained the Lhari boy's hands.

"Bartol, what happened?"

Bart explained. Ringg tried to move, but fell limply back.

"Weren't you hurt? I thought I heard you cry out."

"A cut or two, but nothing serious," Bart said. "I think the hail's stopped. Lie still, I'd better go back to the ship and get help."

"Give me a hand and I can walk," Ringg said, but when he tried to sit up, he flinched, and Bart said, "You'd better lie still." He knew that head injuries should be kept very quiet; he was almost afraid to leave Ringg for fear the Lhari boy would have another delirious fit and hurt himself, but there was no help for it.

The hail had stopped, and the piled heaps were already melting, but it was bitterly cold. Bart wrapped himself in the silvery cloak, glad of its warmth, and struggled back across the slushy, ice-strewn meadow that had been so pink and flowery in the sunshine. The Swiftwing, a monstrous dark egg looming in the twilight, seemed like home. Bart felt the heavenly warmth close around him with a sigh of pure relief, but the Second Officer, coming up the hatchway, stopped in consternation:

"You're covered with blood! The hailstorm—"

"I'm all right," Bart said, "but Ringg's been hurt. You'll need a stretcher." Quickly, he explained. "I'll come with you and show you—"

"You'll do no such thing," the officer said. "You look as if you'd been caught out in a meteor shower, feathertop! We can find the place. You go and have those cuts attended to, and—what's wrong with your wrist? Broken?"

Bart heard, like an echo, the frightening words: Don't break any bones. You won't pass an X-ray.

"It's all right, sir. When I get washed up—"

"That's an order," snapped the officer, "do you think, on this pestilential unlucky planet, we can afford any more bad luck? Metals fatigue, Karol burned so badly the medic thinks he may never use his hand again, and now you and Ringg getting yourselves laid up and out of action? The medic will help me with Ringg; that Mentorian girl can look after you. Get moving!"

He hurried away, and Bart, his head beginning to hurt, walked slowly up the ramp. His whole arm felt numb, and he supported it with his good hand.

In the small infirmary, Karol lay groaning in a bunk, his arm bound in bandages, his head moving from side to side. The Mentorian girl Meta turned, charging a hypo. She looked pale and drawn. She went to Karol, uncovering his other arm, and made the injection; almost immediately the moaning stopped and Karol lay still. Meta sighed and drew a hand over her brow, brushing away feathery wisps that escaped from the cap tied over her hair.

"Bartol? You're hurt? Not more burns, I hope?"

She looks just like a fluffy little kitten, Bart thought incongruously. Fatigue was beginning to blur his reactions.

"Only a few cuts," he said, in Universal, though Meta had spoken Lhari. In his weariness and pain he was homesick for the sound of a familiar word. "Ringg and I were both caught in the hailstorm. He's badly hurt."

"Sit down here."

Bart sat. Meta's hands were skillful and cool as she sponged the blood away from his forehead and sprayed it with some pleasantly cold, mint-smelling antiseptic. Bart leaned back, tireder than he knew, half-closing his eyes.

"That hail must have been enormous; we heard it through the hull. Whatever possessed you to go out into it?"

"It wasn't hailing when we left," Bart said wearily. "The sun was as nice and green as it could be." He bit the words off, realizing he had made a slip, but the girl seemed not to hear, fastening a strip of plastic over a cut. She picked up his wrist. Bart flinched in spite of himself, and Meta nodded. "I was afraid of that; it may be broken. Better let me X-ray it."

"No!" Bart said harshly. "It's all right, I just twisted it. Nothing's broken. Just strap it up."

"It's pretty badly swollen," the girl said, moving it gently. "Does that hurt? I thought so."

Bart set his teeth against a cry. "It's all right, I tell you. Just because it's black and blue—"

He heard her breath jolt out, her fingers clenched painfully on his wounded wrist. She did not hear his cry this time. "And the sun was nice and green," she whispered. "What are you?"

Bart felt himself slip sidewise; he thought for a moment that he would faint where he sat. Terrified, he looked up at Meta. Their eyes met, and she said, hardly moving her pale lips, "Your eyes—they're like mine. Your eyelashes—dark, not white. You're not a Lhari!"

The pain in his wrist suddenly blurred everything else, but Meta suddenly realized she was gripping it; she gave a little, gentle cry, and cradled the abused wrist in her palm.

"No wonder you didn't want it X-rayed," she whispered. Biting her lip, she glanced, terrified, at Karol, unconscious in the bunk. "No, he can't hear us; I gave him a heavy shot of hypnin, poor fellow."

"Go ahead," Bart said bitterly, "yell for your keepers."

Her gray eyes blazed at him for a moment; then, gently, she laid his wrist on the table, went to the infirmary door and locked it on the inside. She turned around, her face white; even her lips had lost their color. "Who are you?" she whispered.

"Does it matter now?"

Shocked comprehension swept over her face. "You don't think I'd tell them," she whispered. "I heard talk, in the Procyon port, of a spy that had managed to get through on a Lhari ship." Her face twisted. "You—you must know about the man on the Multiphase, you know they'll—make sure I can't—hide anything dangerous to the Lhari at the end of the voyage."

"Meta—" concern for her swept over him—"what will they do to you when they find out that you know and—didn't tell?"

Her gray eyes were wide as a kitten's. "Why, nothing. The Lhari would never hurt anyone, would they?"

Brainwashed? He set his mouth grimly. "I hope you never find out different."

"Why would they need to?" she asked, reasonably. "They could just erase the memory. I never heard of a Lhari actually hurting anyone. But something like this—" She wavered, looking at him. "You look so much like a Lhari! How was it done? How could they do it? Poor fellow, you must be the—the loneliest man in the Universe!"

Her voice was compassionate. Bart felt his throat tighten, and had the awful feeling that he was going to cry. He reached with his good hand for hers, seeking the comfort of a human touch, but she flinched instinctively away.

He was a monster to this pretty girl....

"It looks so real," she said helplessly. "Yes, now I can see, you have tiny moons at the base of the nail, and the Lhari don't." Her face worked. "It's—it's horrifying! How could you—"

There was a noise in the corridor. Meta gasped and ran to unlock the door, stood back as the medic and the Second Officer came in, staggering under Ringg's weight. Carefully, they put him into a bunk. The medic straightened, shaking his crest.

"Did you get that wrist taken care of, Bartol?"

Meta stepped between Bart and the officer, reaching for a roll of bandage. "I'm working on it now, rieko mori," she said. "It only wants strapping up." But her fingers trembled as she wound the gauze, pulling each fold tight.

"How's—Ringg?"

"Needs quiet," grunted the medic, "and a few sutures. Lucky you got him under cover when you did."

Ringg said weakly from his bunk, "Bartol saved my life. I can think of plenty who'd have run for cover, instead of staying out in that stuff long enough to drag me inside. Thanks, shipmate."

Meta's hand, with a swift hard pressure, lingered on Bart's shoulder as she cut the bandage and fastened the end. "I don't think that will bother you much now," she whispered, fleetingly. "I didn't dare say it was broken or they'd insist on X-rays. If it hurts I'll get you something later for the pain. If you keep it strapped up tight—"

"It will do," Bart said aloud. The tight bandage made it feel a little better, but he felt sick and dizzy, and when the medic turned and saw him, the officer said brusquely "Watch off for you, Bartol. I'll fix the sign-out sheet, but you go to your cabin and get yourself at least four hours of sleep. That's an order."

Bart stumbled out of the cabin with relief. Safe in his own quarters, he flung himself down on his bunk, shaking all over. He'd come safely through one more nightmare, one more terror—for the moment! Had he put Meta in danger, too? Was there no end to this ceaseless fear? Not only for himself, but for others, the innocent bystanders who stumbled into plots they did not understand?

You're doing this for the stars. It's bigger than your fear. It's bigger than you are, or any of the others....

He was beginning to think it was a lot too big for him.

Chapter Ten

The green-sun Meristem lay far behind them. Karol's burns had healed; only a faint pattern on Ringg's forehead showed where six stitches had closed the ugly wound in his skull. Bart's wrist, after a few days of nightmarish pain when he tried to pick up anything heavy, had healed. Two more warp-drive shifts through space had taken the Swiftwing far, far out to the rim of the known galaxy, and now the great crimson coal of Antares burned in their viewports.

Antares had twelve planets, the outermost of which—far away now, at the furthest point in its orbit from the point of the Swiftwing's entry into the system—was a small captive sun. No larger than the planet Earth, it revolved every ninety years around its huge primary.

Small as it was, it was blazingly blue-white brilliant, and had a tiny planet of its own. After their stop on Antares Seven—the largest of the inhabited planets in this system, where the Lhari spaceport was located—they would make a careful orbit around the great red primary, and land on the tiny worldlet of the blue-white secondary before leaving the Antares system.

As Bart watched Antares growing in the viewports, he felt a variety of emotions. On the one hand, he was relieved that as his voyage in secrecy neared its official destination, he had as yet not incurred unmasking.

But he felt uncertain about his father's co-conspirators. Would they return him to human form and send him back to Vega, his part ended? Or would they, unthinkably, demand that he go on into the Lhari Galaxy? What would he do, if they did?

At one moment he entertained fantasies of going on into the Lhari worlds, returning victorious with the secret of their fueling location, or of the star-drive itself. At another, he could not wait to be free of it all. He longed for the society of his own people, yet ached to think that this voyage between the stars must end so soon.

They made planetfall at the largest Lhari spaceport Bart had seen; as always, the Second Officer was the first to go through Decontam and ashore, returning with exchanged mail and messages for the Swiftwing's crew. He laughed when he gave Bartol a sealed packet. "So you're not quite the orphan we've always thought!"

Bart took it, his heart suddenly pounding, and walked away through the groups of officers and crew eagerly debating how they would spend their port leave. He knew what it would be.

It was on the letterhead of Eight Colors, and it contained no message. Only an address—and a time.

He slipped away unobserved to the Mentorian part of the ship to borrow a cloak from Meta. She did not ask why he wanted it, and stopped him when he would have told her. "I'd—rather not know."

She looked very small and very scared, and Bart wished he could comfort her, but he knew she would shrink from him, repelled and horrified by his Lhari skin, hair, claws.

Yet she reached for his hand, gripping it hard in her own dainty one. "Bartol, be careful," she whispered, then stopped. "Bartol—that's a Lhari name. What's your real one?"

"Bart. Bart Steele."

"Good luck, Bart." There were tears in her gray eyes.

With the blue cloak folded around his face, hands tucked in the slits at the side, he felt almost like himself. And as the strange crimson twilight folded down across the streets, laden with spicy smells and little, fragrant gusts of wind, he almost savored the sense of being a conspirator, of playing for high stakes in a network of intrigue between the stars. He was off on an adventure, and meant to enjoy it.

The address he had been given was a lavish estate, not far from the spaceport, across a little gleaming lake that shimmered red, indigo, violet in the crimson sunset, surrounded by a low wall of what looked like purple glass. Bart, moving slowly through the gate, felt that eyes were watching him, and forced himself to walk with slow dignity.

Up the path. Up a low flight of black-marble stairs. A door swung open and shut again, closing out the red sunset, letting him into a room that seemed dim after the months of Lhari lights. There were three men in the room, but his eyes were drawn instantly to one, standing against an old-fashioned fireplace.

He was very tall and quite thin, and his hair was snow-white, though he did not look old. Bart's first incongruous thought was, He'd make a better Lhari than I would. His firm, commanding voice told Bart at once that this was the man in charge. "You are Bartol?" He extended his hand.

Bart took it—and found himself gripped in a judo hold. The other two men, leaping to place behind him, felt all over his body, not gently.

"No weapons, Montano."

"Look here—"

"Save it," Montano said. "If you're the right person, you'll understand. If not, you won't have much time to resent it. A very simple test. What color is that divan?"

"Green."

"And those curtains?"

"Darker green, with gold and red figures."

The men released him, and the white-haired man smiled.

"So you actually did it, Steele! I thought for sure the code message was a fake." He stepped back and looked Bart over from head to foot, whistling. "Raynor Three is a genius! Claws and everything! What a deuce of a risk to take though!"

"You know my name," Bart said, "but who are you?"

Suspicion came back into the dark eyes. "Does that Mentorian cloak mean—you've lost your memories, too?"

"No," said Bart, "it's simpler than that. I'm not Rupert Steele. I'm—" his voice caught—"I'm his son."

The man looked startled and shocked. "I suppose that means Rupert is dead. Dead! It came a little before he expected it, then. So you're Bart." He sighed. "My name's Montano. This is Hedrick, and I suppose you recognize Raynor Two."

Bart blinked. It was the same face, but it was not grim like Raynor One's, nor expressive and kindly like that of Raynor Three. This one just looked dangerous.

"But sit down," Montano said with a wave of his hand, "make yourself comfortable."

Hedrick relieved Bart of his cloak; Raynor Two put a cup of some steaming drink in his hand, passed him a tray of small hot fried things that tasted crisp and delicious. Bart relaxed, answering questions. How old? Only seventeen? And you came all alone on a Lhari ship, working your way as Astrogator? I must say you've got guts, kid! It was dangerously like the fantasy he had invented. But Montano interrupted at last.

"All right, this isn't a party and we haven't all night. I don't suppose Bart has either. Enough time wasted. Since you walked into this, young Steele, I take it you know what our plans are, after this?"

Bart shook his head. "No. Raynor Three sent me to call off your plans, because of my father—"

"That sounds like Three," interrupted Raynor Two. "Entirely too squeamish!"

Montano said irritably, "We couldn't have done anything without a man on the Swiftwing, and you know it. We still can't. Bart, I suppose you know about Lharillis."

"Not by that name."

"Your next stop. The planetoid of the captive sun. That little hunk of bare rock out there is the first spot the Lhari visited in this galaxy—even before Mentor. It's an inferno of light from that little blue-white sun, so of course they love it—it's just like home to them. When they found that the inner planets of Antares were inhabited, they built their spaceport here, so they'd have a better chance at trade." Montano scowled fiercely.

"But they wanted that little worldlet. So we went all over it to be sure there were no rare minerals there, and finally leased it to them, a century at a time. They mine the place for some kind of powdered lubricant that's better than graphite—it's all done by robot machinery, no one's stationed there. Every time a Lhari ship comes through this system they stop there, even though there's nothing on Lharillis except a landing field and some concrete bunkers filled with robot mining machinery. They'll stop there on the way out of this system—and that's where you come in. We need you on board, to put the radiation counter out of commission."

He took a chart from a drawer, spread it out on a table top. "The simplest way would be to cut these two wires. When the Lhari land, we'll be there, waiting for them. On board the Lhari ship, there must be full records—coordinates of their home world, of where they go for their catalyst fuel—all that."

Bart whistled. "But won't the crew defend the ship? You can't fight energon-ray guns!"

Montano's face was perfectly calm. "No. We won't even try." He handed Bart a small strip of pale-yellow plastic.

"Keep this out of sight of the Mentorians," he said. "The Lhari won't be able to see the color, of course. But when it turns orange, take cover."

"What is it?"

"Radiation-exposure film. It's exactly as sensitive to radiation as you are. When it starts to turn orange, it's picking up radiation. If you're aboard the ship, get into the drive chambers—they're lead-lined—and you'll be safe. If you're out on the surface, you'll be all right inside one of the concrete bunkers. But get under cover before it turns red, because by that time every Lhari of them will be stone-cold dead."

Bart let the strip of plastic drop, staring in disbelief at Montano's cold, cruel face. "Kill them? Kill a whole shipload of them? That's murder!"

"Not murder. War."

"We're not at war with the Lhari! We have a treaty with them!"

"The Federation has, because they don't dare do anything else," Montano said, his face taking on the fanatic's light, "but some of us dare do something, some of us aren't going to sit forever and let them strangle all humanity, hold us down, let us die! It's war, Bart, war for economic survival. Do you suppose the Lhari would hesitate to kill anyone if we did anything to hurt their monopoly of the stars? Or didn't they tell you about David Briscoe, how they hunted him down like an animal—"

"But how do we know that was Lhari policy, and not just—some fanatic?" Bart asked suddenly. He thought of the death of the elder Briscoe, and as always he shivered with the horror of it, but for the first time it came to him: Briscoe had provoked his own death. He had physically attacked the Lhari—threatened them, goaded them to shoot him down in self-defense! "I've been on shipboard with them for months. They're not wanton murderers."

Raynor Two made a derisive sound. "Sounds like it might be Three talking!"

Hedrick growled, "Why waste time talking? Listen, young Steele, you'll do as you're told, or else! Who gave you the right to argue?"

"Quiet, both of you." Montano came and laid his arm around Bart's shoulders, persuasively. "Bart, I know how you feel. But can't you trust me? You're Rupert Steele's son, and you're here to carry on what your father left undone, aren't you? If you fail now, there may not be another chance for years—maybe not in our lifetimes."

Bart dropped his head in his hands. Kill a whole shipload of Lhari—innocent traders? Bald, funny old Rugel, stern Vorongil, Ringg—

"I don't know what to do!" It was a cry of despair. Bart looked helplessly around at the men.

Montano said, almost tenderly, "You couldn't side with the Lhari against men, could you? Could a son of Rupert Steele do that?"

Bart shut his eyes, and something seemed to snap within him. His father had died for this. He might not understand Montano's reasons, but he had to believe that Montano had them.

"All right," he said, thickly, "you can count on me."

When he left Montano's house, he had the details of the plan, had memorized the location of the device he was to sabotage, and accepted, from Montano, a pair of dark contact lenses. "The light's hellish out there," Montano warned. "I know you're half Mentorian, but they don't even take their Mentorians out there. They're proud of saying no human foot has ever touched Lharillis."

When he got back to the Lhari spaceport, Ringg hailed him. "Where have you been? I hunted the whole port for you! I wouldn't join the party till you came. What's a pal for?"

Bart brushed by him without speaking, disregarding Ringg's surprised stare, and went up the ramp. He reached his own cabin and threw himself down in his bunk, torn in two.

Ringg was his friend! Ringg liked him! And if he did what Montano wanted, Ringg would die.

Ringg had followed him, and was standing in the cabin door, watching him in surprise. "Bartol, is something the matter? Is there anything I can do? Have you had more bad news?"

Bart's torn nerves snapped. He raised his head and yelled at Ringg, "Yes, there is something! You can quit following me around and just let me alone for a change!"

Ringg took a step backward. Then he said, very softly, "Suit yourself, Bartol. Sorry." And noiselessly, his white crest held high, he glided away.

Bart's resolve hardened. Loneliness had done odd things to him—thinking of Ringg, a Lhari, one of the freaks who had killed his father, as a friend! If they knew who he was, they would turn on him, hunt him down as they'd hunted Briscoe, as they'd hunted his father, as they'd hounded him from Earth to Procyon. He put his scruples aside. He'd made up his mind.

They could all die. What did he care? He was human and he was going to be loyal to his own kind.

Chapter Eleven

But although he thought he had settled all the conflict, he found that it returned when he was lying in his bunk, or when he stood in the dome and watched the stars, while they moved through the Antares system toward the captive sun and the tiny planet Lharillis.

It's in my power to give this to all men....

Should a few Lhari stand in his way?

He lay in his bunk brooding, thinking of death, staring at the yellow radiation badge. If you fail, it won't be in our lifetime. He'd have to go back to little things, to the little ships that hauled piddling cargo between little planets, while all the grandeur of the stars belonged to the Lhari. And if he succeeded, Vega Interplanet could spread from star to star, a mighty memorial to Rupert Steele.

One day Vorongil sent for him. "Bartol," he said, and his voice was not unkind, "you and Ringg have always been good friends, so don't be angry about this. He's worried about you—says you spend all your spare time in your bunk growling at him. Is there anything the matter, feathertop?"

He sounded so concerned, so—the word struck Bart with hysterical humor—so fatherly, that Bart wanted insanely to laugh and to cry. Instead he muttered, "Ringg should mind his own business."

"But it's not like that," Vorongil said. "Look, the Swiftwing's a world, young fellow, and a small one. If one being in that world is unhappy, it affects everyone."

Bart had an absurd, painful impulse—to blurt out the incredible truth to Vorongil, and try to get the old Lhari to understand what he was doing.

But fear held him silent. He was alone, one small human in a ship of Lhari. Vorongil was frowning at him, and Bart mumbled, "It's nothing, rieko mori."

"I suppose you're pining for home," Vorongil said kindly. "Well, it won't be long now."

The glare of the captive sun grew and grew in the ports, and Bart's dread mounted. He had, as yet, had no opportunity to put the radiation counter out of order. It was behind a panel in the drive room, and try as he might, he could think of no way to get to it unobserved. Sometimes, in sleepless nights, it seemed that would be the best way. Just let it go. But then the Lhari would detect Montano's ship, and kill Montano and his men.

Did he believe that? He had to believe it. It was the only way he could possibly justify what he was doing.

And then his chance came, as so many chances do when one no longer wants them. The Second Officer met him at the beginning of one watch, saying worriedly, "Bartol, old Rugel's sick—not fit to be on his feet. Do you think you can hold down this shift alone, if I drop in and give you a hand from time to time?"

"I think so," Bart said, carefully not overemphasizing it. The Second Officer, by routine, spent half of his time in the drive room, and half his time down below in Maintenance. When he left, Bart knew he would have at least half an hour, uninterrupted, in the drive room. He ripped open the panel, located the wires and hesitated; he didn't quite dare to cut them outright.

He jerked one wire loose, frayed the other with a sharp claw until it was almost in shreds and would break with the first surge of current, pulled two more connections loose so that they were not making full contact. He closed the panel and brushed dust over it, and when the Second Officer came back, Bart was at his own station.

As Antares fell toward them in the viewport, he found himself worrying about Mentorians. They would be in cold sleep, presumably in a safe part of the ship, behind shielding, or Montano would have made provisions for them. Still, he wished there were a way to warn Meta.

He was not on watch when they came into the planetary field of Lharillis, but when he came on shift, he knew at once that the trouble had been located. The panel was pulled open, the exposed wires hanging, and Ringg was facing old Rugel, shouting, "Listen, Baldy, I won't have you accusing me of going light on my work! I checked those panels eight days ago! Tell me who's going to be opening the panels in here anyhow?"

"No, no," Rugel said patiently, "I'm not accusing you of anything, only being careless, young Ringg. You poke with those buzzing instruments and things, maybe once you tear loose some wires."

Bart remembered he wasn't supposed to know what was going on. "What's this all about?"

It was Rugel who answered. "The radiation counter—the planetary one, not the one we use in space—is out of order. We don't even need it this landing—there's no radiation on Lharillis. If it were the landing gear, now, that would be serious. I'm just trying to tell Ringg—"

"He's trying to say I didn't check it." Ringg was not to be calmed. "It's my professional competence—"

"Forget it," Bart said. "If Rugel isn't sore about it, and if we don't need it for landing, why worry?" He felt like Judas.

"Just take a look at my daybook," Ringg insisted, "I checked and marked it service fit! I tell you, somebody was blundering around, opening panels where they had no business, tore it out by accident, then was too much of a filthy sneak to report it and get it fixed!"

"Bartol was on watch alone one night," said the Second Officer, "but you wouldn't meddle with panels, would you, Bartol?"

Bart set his teeth, steadying his breathing, as Ringg turned hopefully to him. "Bartol, did you—by mistake, maybe? Because if you did, it won't count against your rating, but it means a black mark against mine!"

Bart hid his self-contempt in sudden, tense fury. "No, I didn't! You're going to accuse everybody on the Swiftwing, all the way from me to Vorongil, before you can admit a mistake, aren't you? If you want somebody to blame, look in a mirror!"

"Listen, you!" Ringg's pent-up rage exploded. He seized Bart by the shoulder and Bart moved to throw him off, so that Ringg's outthrust claws raked only his forearm. In pure reflex he felt his own claws flick out; they clinched, closed, scuffled, and he felt his claws rake flesh; half incredulous, saw the thin red line of blood welling from Ringg's cheek.

Then Rugel's arms were flung restrainingly around him, and the Second Officer was wrestling with a furious, struggling Ringg. Bart looked at his red-tipped claws in ill-concealed horror, but it was lost in a general gasp of consternation, for Vorongil had flung the drive room door open, taking in the scene in one blistering glance.

"What's going on down here?"

For the first time, Bart understood Vorongil's reputation as a tyrant. One glance at Ringg's bleeding face and Bart's ripped forearm, and he did not pause for breath for a good fifteen minutes. By the time he finished, Bart felt he would rather Ringg's claws had laid him bleeding to the bone than stand there in the naked contempt of the old Lhari's freezing eyes.

"Half-fledged nestlings trying to do a man's work! So someone forgot the panel, or damaged the panel by mistake—no, not another word," he commanded, as Ringg's crest came proudly up. "I don't care who did what! Any more of this, and the one who does it can try his claws on the captain of the Swiftwing!" He looked ugly and dangerous. "I thought better of you both.

Get below, you squalling kittens! Let me not see your faces again before we land!"

As they went along the corridor, Ringg turned to Bart, apology and chagrin in his eyes. "Look—I never meant to get the Bald One down on us," he said, but Bart kept his face resolutely averted. It was easier this way, without pretense of friendship.

The light from the small captive sun grew more intense. Bart had never known anything like it, and was glad to slip away and put the dark contact lenses into his eyes. They made his eyes appear all enormous, dilated pupil; fearfully, he hoped no one would notice. His arm smarted, and he did not speak to Ringg all through the long, slow deceleration.

When the intercom ordered all crew members to the hatchway, Bart lingered a minute, pinning the yellow radiation badge in a fold of his cloak. A spasm of fear threatened to overwhelm him again, and nightmarish loneliness. He felt agonizingly homesick for his own familiar face. It seemed almost more than he could manage, to step out into the corridor full of Lhari.

It won't be long now.

The hatch opened. Even accustomed, as he was, to Lhari lights, Bart squeezed his eyes shut at the blue-white brilliance that assaulted him now. Then, opening slitted lids cautiously, he found that he could see.

A weirdly desolate scene stretched away before them. Bare, burning sand, strewn with curiously colored rocks, lay piled in strange chaos; then he realized there was an odd, but perceptible geometry to their arrangement. They showed alternate crystal and opaque faces. Old Rugel noted his look of surprise.

"Never been here before? That's right, you've always worked on the Polaris run. Well, those aren't true rocks, but living creatures of a sort. The crystals are alive; the opaque faces are lichens that have something like chlorophyll and can make their food from air and sunlight. The rocks and lichens live in symbiosis. They have intelligence of a sort, but fortunately they don't mind us, or our automatic mining machinery. Every time, though, we find some new lichen that's trying to set up a symbiote cycle with the concrete of our bunkers."

"And every time," Ringg said cheerfully, "somebody—usually me—has to see about having them scraped down and repainted. Maybe someday I'll find a paint the lichens don't like the taste of."

"Going to explore with Ringg?" Rugel asked, and Ringg, always ready to let bygones be bygones, grinned and said, "Sure!" Bart could not face him.

Vorongil stopped and said, "This your first time here, young Bartol? How would you like to visit the monument with me? You can see the machinery on the way back."

Relieved at not having to go with Ringg, he followed the captain, falling into step beside him. They moved in silence, along the smooth stone path.

"The crystal creatures made this road," Vorongil said at last. "I think they read minds a little. There used to be a very messy, rocky desert here, and we used to have to scrabble and scratch our way to the monument. Then one day a ship—not mine—touched down and discovered that there was a beautiful smooth road leading up to the monument. And the lichens never touch that stone—but you probably had all this in school. Excited, Bartol?"

"No—no, sir. Why?"

"Eyes look a bit odd. But who could blame you for being excited? I never come here without remembering Rhazon and his crew on that long jump. The longest any Lhari captain ever made. A blind leap in the dark, remember, Bartol. Through the dark, through the void, with his own crew cursing him for taking the chance! No one had ever crossed between galaxies—and remember, they were using the Ancient Math!"

He paused, and Bart said through a catch of breath. "Quite an achievement." His badge still looked reassuringly yellow.

"You young people have no sense of wonder," Vorongil said. "Not that I blame you. You can't realize what it was like in those days. Oh, we'd had star-travel for centuries, we were beginning to stagnate. And now look at us! Oh, they derided Rhazon—said that even if he did find anyone, any other race, they'd be monsters with whom we could never communicate. But here we have a whole new galaxy for peaceful trade, a new mathematics that takes all the hazard out of space travel, our Mentorian friends and allies." He smiled. "Don't tell the High Council on me, but I think they deserve a lot more credit than most Lhari care to give them. Between ourselves, I think the next Panarch may see it that way."

Vorongil paused. "Here's the monument."

It lay between the crystal columns, tall, of pale blue sandstone, with letters in deep shadow of such contrast that the Lhari could read them: a high, sheer, imposing stele. Vorongil read the words slowly aloud in the musical Lhari language:

"'Here, with thanks to Those who Watch the Great Night, I, Rhazon of Nedrun, raise a stone of memory. Here we first do touch the new worlds. Let us never again fear to face the unknown, trusting that the Mind of All Knowledge still has many surprises in store for all the living.'

"I think I admire courage more than anything there is, Bartol. Who else could have dared it? Doesn't it make you proud to be a Lhari?"

Bart had felt profoundly moved; now he snapped back to awareness of who he was and what he was doing. So only the Lhari had courage? Life has surprises, all right, Captain, he thought grimly.

He glanced down at the badge strip of plastic on his arm. It began to tinge faint orange as he looked, and a chill of fear went over him. He had to get away somehow—get to cover!

He looked round and his fear was almost driven from his mind. "Captain, the rocks! They're moving!"

Vorongil said, unruffled, "Why, so they are. They do, you know; they have intelligence of a sort. Though I've never actually seen them move before, I know they shift places overnight. I wonder what's going on?" They were edging back, the path widening and changing. "Oh, well, maybe they're going to do some more landscaping for us. I once knew a captain who swore they could read his mind."

Bart saw the slow, inexorable deepening of his badge—he had to get away. He tensed, impatient; gripped by fists of panic. Somewhere on this world, Montano and his men were setting up their lethal radiations....

Think of this: a Lhari ship of our own to study, to know how it works, to see the catalyst and find out where it comes from, to read their records and star routes. Now we know we can use it without dying in the warp-drive....

Think of this: to be human again, yet to travel the stars with men of my own race!

It's worth a few deaths!

Even Vorongil? Standing here, talking to him, he might—say it! You talked to him as if he'd been your father! Oh, Dad, Dad, what would you do?

His voice was steady, as he said, "It's very good of you to show me all this, sir, but the other men will call me a slacker. Hadn't I better get to a work detail?"

"Hm, maybe so, feathertop," Vorongil said. "Let me see—well, down this way is the last row of bunkers. See the humps? You can check inside to see if they're full or empty and save us the trouble of exploring if they're all empty. Have a look round inside if you care to—the robot machinery's interesting."

Bart tensed; he had wondered how he'd get hidden inside, but he asked, "Not locked?"

"Locked?" The old Lhari's short, yellowed crest bobbed in surprise. "Why? Who ever comes here but our ships? And what could we do with the stuff but take it back with us? Why locked? You've been on the drift too long—among those thieving humans! It's time you got back to live among decent folk again. Well, go along."

The sting of the words stiffened Bart as he took his leave. The color of the badge seemed deeper orange....

When it's red, you're dead.

It's true. The Lhari don't steal. They don't even seem to understand dishonesty.

But they lied—lied to us all....

Knowing what we were like, maybe! That we'd steal their ships, their secrets, their lives!

The deepening color of the badge seemed the one visible thing in a strange glaring world. He walked along the row of bunkers, realizing he need not check if they were full or empty—the Lhari wouldn't live long enough to harvest their better-than-graphite lubricant. They'd be dead.

The last bunker was empty. He looked at his orange badge and stepped inside, heart pounding so loudly he thought it was an external sound—it was an external sound, a step.

"Don't move one inch," said a voice in Universal, and Bart froze, trembling. He looked cautiously round.

Montano stood there, spacesuited, his head bare, dark contact lenses blurring his eyes. And in his hand a drawn blaster was held level—trained straight at Bart's heart.

Chapter Twelve

After the first moment of panic, Bart realized Montano could not tell him from a Lhari. He remained motionless. "It's me, Montano—Bart Steele."

The man lowered the weapon and put it away. "You nearly got yourself cut down," he said. "Did you make it all right?" He crossed behind Bart, inspecting the fastenings of the bunker.

"It's just luck I didn't shoot you first and ask questions afterward." Montano drew a deep breath and sat down on the concrete floor. "Anyway, we're safe in here. We've got about half an hour before the radiation will reach lethal intensity. It has a very short half-life, though; only about twelve minutes. If we spend an hour in here, we'll be safe enough. Did you have any trouble putting the radiation counter out of commission?"

So in half an hour they would all be dead. Ringg, Rugel, Captain Vorongil. Two dozen Lhari, all dead so that Montano could have a Lhari ship to play with.

And what then? More killing, more murder? Would Montano start killing everyone who tried to get the secret of the drive from him? The Lhari had the star-drive; maybe it belonged to them, maybe not. Maybe humans had a right to have it, too. But this wasn't the right way. Maybe they didn't deserve it.

He turned to look at Montano. The man was leaning back, whistling softly through his teeth. He felt like telling Montano that he couldn't go through with it. He started to speak, then stopped, his blood icing over.

If I try to argue with him, I'll never get out of here alive. It means too much to him.

Do I just salve my conscience with that then? Sit here and let them die?

With a shock of remembrance, it came to Bart that he had a weapon. He was armed, this time, with the energon-beam that was part of his uniform. Montano had evidently forgotten it. Could he kill Montano? Even to save two dozen Lhari?

He reached hesitantly toward the beam-gun, quickly thumbed the catch down to the lowest point, which was simple shock. He froze as Montano looked in his direction, hand out of sight under his cloak.

"How many Lhari on board?"

"Twenty-three, and three Mentorians."

"Anyone apt to be behind shielding—say, in the drive chamber?"

"No, I think they're all outside."

Montano nodded, idly. "Then we won't have to worry."

Bart slipped his hand toward his weapon. Montano saw the movement, cocked his head in question; then, as understanding flashed over his face, his hand darted to his own gun. But Bart had pressed the charge of his, and Montano slumped over without a cry. He looked so limp that Bart gasped. Was he dead? Hastily he fumbled the lax hand for a pulse. After a long, endless moment he saw Montano's chest twitch and knew the man was breathing.

Well, Montano would be safe here in the bunker. Hastily, Bart looked at his timepiece. Half an hour before the radiation was lethal—for the Lhari. Was it already, for him? Shakily, he unfastened the door. He ran out into the glare, seeing as he ran that his badge was tinged with an ever-darkening, gold, orange....

Montano had said there was a safety margin, but maybe he was wrong, maybe all Bart would accomplish would be his own death! He ran back along the line of bunkers, his heart pounding with his racing feet. Two crewmen came along the line, young white-crested Lhari from the other watch. He gasped, "Where is the captain?"

"Down that way—what's wrong, Bartol?" But Bart was gone, his muscles aching with the unaccustomed effort inside gravity. Putting on speed, he saw the tall, austere shape of Vorongil, his banded cloak dark against the glaring light. Vorongil turned, startled, at the sound of his running feet.

Suddenly, Bart realized that he was still holding his energon-ray. In shock and revulsion, he dropped it at Vorongil's feet.

"Captain, go warn the men! They'll all be dead in half an hour! There are lethal radiations—"

"What? Are you sunstruck?"

Bart stopped cold. Never once had it crossed his mind what he would say to Vorongil or how he would make the captain believe his story, without revealing Montano. He started to hold up his badge, realized the Lhari captain could not see color, and dropped it again, while Vorongil bent over to pick up the fallen gun. "Are you sunstruck or mad, Bartol? What's this babble?"

"Captain, everybody on the Swiftwing—"

"And speak Lhari!" Vorongil demanded, and Bart realized that in his excitement he had been shouting in Universal. He drew a long, deep breath.

"Captain, there are lethal radiations being released here," he said. "You have just barely half an hour to gather all the men and get them behind shielding."

"The radiation counter is out of order," Vorongil remarked, unruffled. "How can you possibly know—"

Bart stood in despair. Could he say, A ship has landed here? Could he say, Check that bunker? Even if Montano was a would-be murderer, he was human, and Bart could not betray him to the Lhari. There had been too much betrayal. His voice rose in sudden hysteria.

"Captain, there's no time! I tell you, you'll all be dead if you don't believe me! Get the men into the ship! Get them behind shielding and then check my story! I'm not—" he had gone this far, he might as well go the whole way—"I'm not a Lhari!"

"What?"

One of the crewmen came dashing up, his crest sweat-streaked. "Captain! Rugel has collapsed! We don't know what's wrong with him."

"Radiation sickness," said Bart, and Vorongil reached out, catching his shoulder in a cruel taloned grip. Bart said desperately "I'm not a Lhari! I signed on in disguise—I knew they meant to take the ship, but I can't let you all die.

"How can I make you believe me? Here—" In desperation, Bart reached up. Pain stabbed his eyeballs, fierce, blinding, as he pulled out one of the contact lenses. He could not see the captain's face through the light, but suddenly two Lhari were holding his arms. The fear of death was on Bart, but it no longer mattered. He saw through watering eyes the ever-deepening orange of the badge disappearing.

"Here," he said, tearing at it, "radiation. You must be able to see how dark it is. Even if it's just darkness...."

Suddenly Vorongil was shouting, but Bart could not hear. Two men were dragging him along. They hustled him up the ramp of the ship. He could see again, but his eyes were blurred, and he felt sick, colors spinning before his eyes, a nauseated ringing in his head.

At first he thought it was his ears ringing; then he made out the rising, shrieking wail and fall of the emergency siren, steps running, shouting voices, the slow clang of the doors. Someone was pushing at him, babbling words in Lhari, but he heard them through an ever-increasing distance: Vorongil's face bent over his, only a blurred crimson blob that flashed away like a vanishing star in the viewport. It flamed out into green darkness, vanished, and Bart fell through what seemed to be a bottomless chasm of starless night.

When he woke, acceleration had its crushing hand on his chest. He tried to move, discovered that he was strapped hard into a bunk, and fainted again.

Suddenly the pressure was gone and he was lying at ease on the smooth sheets of a hospital bunk. His eyes were covered with a light bandage, and there was a sharp pain in his left arm. He tried to move it and found it was tied down.

"I think he's coming round," said Vorongil's voice.

"Yes, and a lot too soon for me," said a bitter voice which Bart recognized as that of the ship's medic. "Freak!"

"Listen, Baldy," said Vorongil, "whoever he is, he could have been blinded or killed. You wouldn't be alive now if it wasn't for that freak, as you call him. Bartol, can you hear me? How much light can your eyes stand?"

"As much as any Mentorian." Bart found he could move his right arm, and twitched the bandage away. Vorongil and the medic stood over him; in the other infirmary bunk a form was lying, covered with a white sheet. Sickly, Bart wondered if they had found Montano. Vorongil followed the direction of his eyes.

"Yes," he said, and his voice held deep bitterness, "poor old Rugel is dead. He didn't get much of the radiation, but his heart wouldn't stand it, and gave out." He bowed his head. "He was bald in the service of the ships when my crest was new-sprouted," he said in deep grief.

Bart felt the shock of that, even through his own fear. He looked down at his left arm. It was strapped to a splint, and fluid was dripping slowly into the vein there.

Vorongil nodded. "I expect you feel pretty sick. You got a good dose of radiation yourself, but we've given you a couple of transfusions—one of the Mentorians matched your blood type, fortunately. It was a close call."

The medic was looking down in ill-disguised curiosity. "Fantastic," he said. "I don't suppose you'd tell me who changed your looks. I admit I wouldn't believe it until I had a look at your foot bones under the fluoroscope."

Vorongil said quietly, "Bartol—I don't suppose that's your real name—why did you do it?"

"I couldn't see you all die, sir," Bart said, not expecting them to believe him. "No more than that."

The medic said roughly in Lhari, "It's a trick, sir, no more. A trick to make us trust him!"

"Why would he risk his own life then?" Vorongil asked. "No, it's more than that." He hesitated. "We checked the bunkers—in radiation suits—before we took off. We found a man in one of them."

"Was he dead?" Bart whispered.

"No," Vorongil said quietly.

"Thank God!" It was a heartfelt explosion. Then, apprehensively, "Or did you kill him?"

"What do you think we are?" Vorongil said incredulously. "Indeed no. His own men have probably found him by now. I don't imagine he got half as much radiation as you did."

Bart surveyed the needle in his arm. "Why are you taking all this trouble if I'm going to be put out of the way?"

"You must have some funny ideas about us," Vorongil said shaking his head. "That would be a fine way to reward you for saving all of our lives. No, you're not going to be killed."

"If I had my way—" the old medic began, and suddenly Vorongil flew into a rage. "Get out!"

The medic went stiffly through the door, and Vorongil stood gazing down at Bart, shaking his yellowed crest. "I don't know what to say to you. It was a brave thing you did, but perhaps no braver than you've done all along. Are you a Mentorian?"

"Only half."

"Strange," Vorongil said, looking into space, "that I could talk to you as I did by the monument, and you knew what I meant. But, yes, you would understand." Abruptly, he recalled himself, and his voice was thin and cold.

"I haven't quite decided what to do. I haven't spoken of this to the crew yet; the fewer who know about this, the better. I told them you got a heavy dose of radiation, and you're too sick to see visitors." He sounded kinder when he said, "It's true, you know. It won't hurt you to get your strength back."

He went out, and Bart wondered, Get my strength back for what? He lay back, feeling weaker than he realized. It was a relief to know he wasn't going to be killed out of hand. And somehow he didn't believe he was going to be killed at all.

It wasn't like being a prisoner. The medic brought him plenty of food, urging him to eat—"You need plenty of protein after radiation burns"—and if he stayed in the bunk, it was only because he felt too weak to get up. Actually he was suffering from delayed emotional shock, as well as from radiation. He was content to let things drift.

Inevitably, the time came when he had to think about what he had done. He had betrayed Montano, he had been false to the men who sent him.

"But they don't know the Lhari," his conscience replied, justifying what he had done.

You sided with the Lhari against your own people. You spoilt our chances of learning about the Lhari fuel catalyst.

"I've done something better than stealing a secret by stealth. I've proved that humans and Lhari can communicate, that they can trust each other. It's only their looks that are strange. A kind, generous man is a kind generous man, whether his name is Raynor Three or Vorongil."

But who's going to know it?

"I know it. And truth comes out, sooner or later. Somehow, a better understanding between man and Lhari will come from this."

Secure in the knowledge, he turned over and went peacefully to sleep.

When he woke again, he felt better. The Mentorian girl, Meta, was sitting quietly between the bunks, watching him. He started to turn over, flinched at the pain in his arm.

"Yes," she said, "we're giving you one last transfusion. Plasma, this time. It's Lhari, but if you know that much, you know it won't hurt you." She came and inspected the needle in his wrist, and Bart caught her hand with his free one. "Meta, does anyone else know?"

She looked down with a troubled smile. "I don't think so. I was off watch, waiting for cold-sleep—we're just about to make the long jump—when Vorongil came to my quarters. I was startled almost out of my wits. He asked if I could keep a secret; then he told me about you. Oh, Bart!" Her small soft hand closed convulsively on his, "I was so afraid! I knew they wouldn't kill you, but I was afraid!"

Yet they had killed David Briscoe, Bart thought, and hunted down two of his friends. It was the only thing he couldn't square with his perception of the Lhari. It didn't fit. He could understand that they had shot down the robotcab with Edmund Briscoe in it, in pure self-defense; and that knowledge had taken off the edge of the horror. But the death of young Briscoe and everyone he had talked to could not be explained away.

"You seem very sure they wouldn't have killed me, Meta," he said, carefully clasping his hand around hers.

"They wouldn't," she affirmed. "But they could—make you forget—"

A small chill went over Bart. He let go of her hand and lay staring bleakly at the wall. He supposed that was his probable fate: remembering the tragic tone of Raynor Three when he said I won't remember you, he gritted his teeth, feeling his face twist convulsively. Meta, watching, misunderstood.

"Arm hurting? I'll have that needle out of your vein in a few minutes now."

When she had freed his arm and put away the apparatus, she came to his side. "Bart, how did it happen? How did they find you out?"

Suddenly, the longing for human contact was too much for Bart, and the knowledge of his secret intolerable. The Lhari could find out what he knew, if they wanted to know, very simply; he was in their power. It didn't matter any more.

The telling of the story took a long time, and when he finished, Meta's soft small kitten-face was compassionate.

"I'm glad you—decided what you did," she whispered. "It's what a Mentorian would have done. I know that other races call us slaves of the Lhari. We aren't. We're working in our own way to show the Lhari that human beings can be trusted. The other peoples—they hold away from the Lhari, fighting them with words even though they're afraid to fight them with weapons, carrying on the war that they're afraid to fight!

"Did it ever occur to you—all the peoples of all the planets keep saying, We're as good as the Lhari, but only the Mentorians are willing to prove it? Bart, a Lhari ship can't get along in our galaxy without Mentorians any more! It may be slower than trying to take the warp-drive by force, or stealing it by spying, but when we learn to endure it, I have faith that we'll get it!"

Bart, although moved by Meta's philosophy, couldn't quite share it. It still seemed to him that the Mentorians were lacking in something—independence, maybe, or drive.

"I wasn't thinking about anything like that," he said honestly. "It was simply that I couldn't let them die. After all—" he was speaking more to himself than to the girl—"it's their star-drive. They found it. And they've given us star-trade, and star-travel, cheaply and with profit to both sides. I hope we'll get the star-drive someday. But if we got it by mass murder, it would sow the seeds of a hatred between men and Lhari that would never end. It wouldn't be worth it, Meta. Nothing would be worth that. We've got enough hate already."

Bart was still in his bunk, but beginning to fret at staying there, when the familiar trembling of Acceleration Two started to run through the ship. It was, by now, so familiar to him that he hardly gave it a second thought, but Meta panicked.

"What's happening? Bart, what is it? Why are we under acceleration again?"

"Shift to warp," he said without thinking, and her face went deathly white. "So that's it," she whispered. "Vorongil—no wonder he wasn't worried about what I would find out from you or what you knew." She drew herself together in her chair, a miserable, shrunken, terrified little figure, bravely trying to control her terror.

Then she held out her hands to Bart. "I'm—I'm ashamed," she whispered. "When you've been so brave, I shouldn't be afraid to die."

"Meta, what's the matter? What are you afraid of?" It suddenly swept over Bart what she meant and what she feared. "But don't you understand, Meta?" he exclaimed, "Humans can live through the warp-drive! No drugs, no cold-sleep—Meta, I've done it dozens of times!"

"But you're a Lhari!" It burst from her, uncontrollable. She stopped, looked at him in consternation. He smiled, bitterly.

"No, Meta, they didn't do a thing to my internal organs, to my brain, to the tissues of my body. Just a little plastic surgery on my hands, my feet and my face. Meta, there's nothing to be afraid of—nothing," he repeated.

She twisted her small hands together. "I'm—trying to—to believe that," she whispered, "but all my life I've known—"

The screaming whine in the ship gripped them with the strange, clawing lassitude and discomfort. Bart, gasping under it, heard the girl moan, saw her slump lax in her chair, half fainting. Her face was so deathly white that he began seriously to be afraid she would die of her fear. Fighting his own agonizing weakness, he pulled himself upright. He reached the girl, dug his claws cruelly into her.

"Girl, get hold of yourself! Fight it! Fight it! The more scared you are, the worse it's going to be!"

She was rigid, trembling, in a trance of terror.

"You rotten little coward," he yelled at her, "snap out of it! Or are all you Mentorians so gutless that you believe any half-baked folk tale the Lhari pass off on you? You and your fine talk about earning the star-drive! What would you do with it after you got it—if you die of fear when you try?"

"Oh! You—!" She flung her head back, her eyes blazing with rage. "Anything you can do, I can do, too!" He saw life flowing back into her face, and the trembling now was with fury, not fear; she was fighting the pain, the crawling itch in her nerve ends, the terrible sense of draining disorganization.

Bart felt his hold on himself breaking. He whispered hoarsely, "That's the girl—don't be scared if I—black out for a minute." He held on to consciousness with his last courage, afraid if he fainted, the girl would collapse again.

She reached for him, and Bart, starved for some human touch, drew her into his arms. They clung together, and he felt her wet face against his own, the softness of her trembling hands. She was still crying a little. Then the blackness closed on him, as if endless, and the gray blur of warp-drive peak blotted his brain into nothingness.

He came out of it to feel her cheek soft against his, her head trustfully on his shoulder. He said huskily, "All right, Meta?"

"I'm fine," she murmured, shakily. He tightened his hands a little, realizing that for the first time in months he had physically forgotten his Lhari disguise, that Meta had given him this priceless reassurance that he was human. But, as if suddenly aware of it again, she looked up at him and drew hesitantly away.

"Don't—Meta, am I so horrible to you then? So—repulsive?"

"No, it's only—" she bit her lip—"it's just that the Lhari are—I can't quite explain it."

"Different," Bart finished for her. "At first I was repelled—physically repelled by myself, and by them. It was like living among weird animals, and being one of the animals. And then, one day, Ringg was just another kid. He had gray skin and long claws and white hair, just the way I once had pinkish skin and short fingernails and reddish hair, but the difference wasn't that I was human inside and he wasn't. If you skinned Ringg, and skinned me, we'd be almost identical. And all of a sudden then, Ringg and Vorongil and all the rest were men to me. Just people. I thought you Mentorians, after living with the Lhari all these years, would feel that."

She said in slow wonder, "We've lived and worked side by side with them all these years, yet kept so apart! I've defended the Lhari to you, yet it took you to explain them to me!"

His arm was still round her, her head still lying on his shoulder. Bart was just beginning to wonder if he might kiss her when the infirmary door opened and Ringg stood in the doorway, staring at them with surprise, shock and revulsion. Bart realized, suddenly, how it must look to Ringg—who certainly shared Meta's prejudice—but even as he comprehended it, Ringg's face altered. Meta slipped from Bart's arms and rose, but Ringg came slowly a step into the room.

"I—remembered you had a bad reaction, to warp-drive," he said. "I came to see if you were all right. I would never have believed—but I'm beginning to guess. There was always something about you, Bartol." He shut the door behind him and stood against it. His voice lowered almost to a whisper, he said, "You're not Lhari, are you?"

"Vorongil knows," Bart said.

Ringg nodded. "That day on Lharillis. The crew was talking, but only one or two of them really know what happened. There are a dozen rumors. I wanted to see you. They said you were sick with radiation burns—"

"I was."

Ringg raised his hand, absently, to the still-puckered mark on his cheek, saw Bart watching him and smiled.

"You're not worrying about that fight? Forget it, friend. If anything, I admire someone who can use his claws—especially if, as I begin to suspect, they're not his." He leaned over, his hand lightly on Bart's shoulder. "I don't forget so easily. You saved my life, remember? And you're a hero on the ship for warning us all. Are you really human? Why not get rid of the disguise?"

Bart laughed wryly. "It won't come off," he said, and explained.

Ringg raised his hands to his own face curiously. "I wonder what sort of human I'd make?" He looked at Meta's small fingers. "Not that I'd ever have the nerve. But then, it's no surprise to anyone that you have courage, Bartol."

"You seem to accept it—"

"It's a shock," said Ringg honestly, "it scares me a little. But I'm remembering the friendship. That was real. As far as I'm concerned, it still is real."

Chapter Thirteen

Ringg was still bending over Meta's hand when Vorongil came into the cabin. He started to speak, then noticed Ringg. "I might have known," he growled, "if there was anything to find out, you'd find it."

"Shall I go, rieko mori?"

"No, stay. You'll find it out some way or other, you might as well get it right the first time. But first of all—are you all right, Meta?"

Her chin went up, defiantly. "Yes. And why have you lied to us all these years—all of you?"

Vorongil looked mildly startled. "It wasn't exactly a lie. Nine out of ten Lhari captains believe it with all their heart—that humans die in warp-drive. I wasn't sure myself until I heard the debates in Council City, last year."

"But why?"

Vorongil sighed. His eyes rested disconcertingly on Bart. "I presume you know human history," he said, "better than I do. The Lhari have never had a war, in all written history. Quite frankly, you terrified us. It was decided, on the highest summit levels, that we wouldn't give humans too many chances to find out things we preferred to keep to ourselves. The first few ships to carry Mentorians had carried them without cold-sleep, but people forget easily. The truth is buried in the records of those early voyages.

"As the Mentorians grew more important to us, we began to regret the policy, but by that time the Mentorians themselves believed it so firmly that when we tried the experiment of carrying them through the shift into warp-drive, they died of fear—pure suggestion. I tried it with you, Meta, because I knew Bart's presence would reassure you. The others were given an inert sedative they believed to be the cold-sleep drug. How are you feeling, Bart?"

"Fine—but wondering what's going to happen."

"You won't be hurt," Vorongil said, quickly. Then: "You don't believe me, do you?"

"I don't, sir. David Briscoe did what I did, and he's dead. So are three other men."

"Men do strange things from fear—men and Lhari. Your people, as I said before, have a strange history. It scares us. Can you guarantee that some, at least, of your people wouldn't try to come and take the star-drive by force? We left a man on Lharillis who thought nothing of killing twenty-four of us. I suppose the captain of the Multiphase, knowing he had gravely violated Lhari laws, knowing that Briscoe's report might touch off an intergalactic war between men and Lhari—well, I suppose he felt that half a dozen deaths were better than half a million. I'm not defending him. Just explaining, maybe, why he did what he did."

Bart lowered his eyes. He had no answer to that.

"No, you won't be killed. But that's all I can guarantee. My personal feelings have nothing to do with it. You'll have to go to Council Planet with us, and you'll have to be psych-checked there. That is Lhari law—and by treaty with your Federation, it is human law, too. If you know anything dangerous to us, we have a legal right to eliminate those memories before you can be released."

Meta smiled at him, encouragingly, but Bart shivered. That was almost worse than the thought of death.

And the fear grew more oppressive as the ship forged onward toward the home world of the Lhari. And it did not lessen when, after they touched down, he was taken from the ship under guard.

He had only a glimpse, through dark glasses, of the terrible brilliance of the Lhari sun dazzling on crystal towers, before he was hustled into a closed surface car. It whisked him away to a building he did not see from the outside; he was taken up by private elevator to a suite of rooms which might—for all he could tell—have been a suite in a luxury hotel or a lunatic asylum. The walls were translucent, the furniture oddly colored, and so carefully padded that even a homicidal or suicidal person could not have hurt himself or anyone else on it or with it.

Food reached him often enough so that he never got hungry, but not often enough to keep him from being bored between meals, or from brooding. Two enormous Lhari came in to look at him every hour or so, but either they were deaf and dumb, did not understand his dialect of Lhari, or were under orders not to speak to him. It was the most frustrating time of his entire voyage.

One day it ended. A Lhari and a Mentorian came for him and took him down elevators and up stairs, and into a quiet, neutral room where four Lhari were gathered. They sat him in a comfortable chair, and the Mentorian interpreter said gently, with apology:

"Bart Steele, I have been asked to say to you that you will not be physically harmed in any way. This will be much simpler, and will have much less injurious effect on your mind if you cooperate with us. At the same time, I have been asked to remind you that resistance is absolutely useless, and if you attempt it, you will only be treated with force rather than with courtesy."

Bart sat facing them, shaking with humiliation. The thought of resistance flashed through his mind. Maybe he should make them fight for what they got! At least they'd see that all humans weren't like the Mentorians, to sit quietly and let themselves be brainwashed without a word of protest.

He started to spring up, and the hands of his guards tightened, swift and strong, even before his muscles had fully tightened. Bart's head dropped. Cold common sense doused over his brave thoughts. He was uncountable millions of light-years from his own people. He was absolutely alone. Bravery would mean nothing; submission would mean nothing. Would he be more of a man, somehow, if he let his mind be wrecked?

"All right," he muttered, "I won't fight."

"You show your good sense," the Mentorian said quietly. "Give me your left arm, please—or, if you are left-handed, your right. As you prefer."

Deftly, almost painlessly, a needle slid into his arm. Giving in. A dizzying welter of thoughts spun suddenly in his mind. Briscoe. Raynor One and Raynor Three. The net between the stars. Ringg, Vorongil, Meta, his father....

Consciousness slid away.

Years later—he never knew whether it was memory or imagination—it seemed to him that he could reach into that patch of gray and dreamless time and fish out questions and answers whole, the faces of Lhari swelling up suddenly in his eyes and shrinking back into interstellar distance, the sting-smell of drugs, the sound of unexpected voices, odd reflex pains, cobwebs of patchy memories that fitted nowhere else into his life so that he supposed they must go here.

He only knew that there was a time he did not remember and then a time when he began to think there was such a thing as memory, and then a time when he floated without a body, and then another time when the path of every separate nerve in his body seemed to be outlined, a shimmering web in the gray murk. There was a mirror and a face. There were blotchy worms of light like the star-trails of peaking warp-drive through the viewport, colors shifting and receding, a green star, the red eye of Antares.

Then the peak-point faded, his mind began to decelerate and angle slowly down and down into the field of awareness, and he became fuzzily aware that he was lying full length on a sort of couch. He shook his head groggily. It hurt. He sat up. That hurt, too. A hand closed gently around his elbow and he felt the cold edge of a cup against his sore mouth.

"Take a sip of this."

The liquid felt cool on his tongue, evaporating almost before he could swallow; the fumes seemed to mount inside the root of his nose, expanding tremendously inside his head and brain. Abruptly his head was clear, the last traces of gray fuzz gone.

"When you feel able," the Mentorian said courteously, "the High Council will see you."

Bart blinked. As if exploring a sore tooth with his tongue, his mind sought for memories, but they all seemed clear, marshaled in line. The details, clear and unblurred, of his voyage here. His humiliation and resentment against the Lhari. *They could have changed my thinking, my attitudes. They could have made me admire or be loyal to the Lhari. They didn't. I'm still me.*

"I'm ready now." He got up, reeled and had to lean on the Mentorian; his feet did not seem to touch the ground in quite the right way. After a minute he could walk steadily, and followed the Mentorian along a corridor. The Mentorian said into a small grille, "The Vegan Bartol, alias Bart Steele," and after a moment a doorway opened.

Inside a room rose, high, domed, vaulted above his head, whitish opalescent, washed with green. For a moment, while his eyes adjusted to the light, he wondered how the Lhari saw it.

Beyond an expanse of black, glassy floor, he saw a low semicircular table, behind which sat eight Lhari. All wore pale robes with high collars that rose stiffly behind their domed heads; all were old, their faces lined with many wrinkles, and seven of the eight were as bald as the hull of the Swiftwing. Under their eyes he hesitated; then, unexpectedly, pride stiffened his back.

They should have done a better job of brainwashing, if they expected him to skulk in like a scared rabbit! He held his head high and moved across the floor step by steady step, trying not to limp or display that he felt tired or sore.

You're human! Act proud of it!

No one moved until he stood before the semicircle of ancients. Then the youngest, the only one of the eight with some trace of feathery crest on his high gray head, said "Captain Vorongil, you identify this person?"

"I do," Vorongil said, and Bart saw him seated before the high Council. To Bart, the Lhari captain seemed a familiar, almost a friendly face.

"Well, Bart Steele, alias Bartol son of Berihun," said one old Lhari, "what have you to say for yourself?"

Bart stood silent, not moving. What could he say that would not reveal how desperately alone, how young and foolish and frightened he felt? All his brave resolutions seemed to drain away before their old, gnomish faces. Here he'd been thinking of himself as a brave spy, a gallant fighter in humanity's cause and what not. Now he saw himself for what he was; a reckless boy, meddling in affairs too big for him. He lowered his eyes.

"We have read the transcript of your knowledge," said the old Lhari. "There is little in it that we do not know. We are not, of course, concerned with human conspiracies unless they endanger Lhari lives. The Antares authorities will deal with the man Montano for an unauthorized landing on Lharillis, in violation of Federation treaty."

He smiled, his gnome's face breaking into a million tiny cracks like a piece of gray-glazed pottery. "Bartol, or whatever you call yourself, you are a brave young man. I suppose you are afraid we will block your memories, or your ability to speak of them?"

Bart nodded, gulping. Did the old Lhari read his mind?

"A year ago we might have done so. Captain Vorongil, you will be interested to know that we have discussed this in Council, and your recommendations have been taken. The secret that humans can endure star-drive has outlived its usefulness. For good or ill, it is secret no longer. We cannot possibly eliminate all the old records, or the enterprising people who hunt them out.

"The captain who had David Briscoe killed, under the mistaken notion that this would excuse his own negligence in letting Briscoe stow away on his ship, is undergoing psychotherapy and may eventually recover.

"As for the rest—Bart Steele, you know nothing that is a danger to us. You do not know the coordinates of our world, or even in which galaxy it is located. You do not know where we secure the catalyst your people seek. In fact, you know nothing that is not soon to become common knowledge. In view of that, we have decided not to interfere with your memories."

"Talk as much as you like," added another of the ancients, "and may your memories of this voyage help in understanding between the Lhari and other human races. Good fortune to you." And he was smiling.

"There is another side to this," said a third, more sternly and gravely. "You have broken a treaty between Lhari and man. We have dealt with you as the laws required; now your own people must do so. You must return with the Swiftwing to the planet where the violation originated—" he consulted a memorandum—"Procyon Alpha. There you and the man Raynor Three will face charges of unlawful conspiracy to board a Lhari ship, in violation of

Intergalactic Trade treaties. Captain Vorongil, will you be responsible for him?"

So I've lost, Bart thought drearily. I didn't even learn anything important enough for them to suppress. There was a strange wounded pride in this; after all his trouble, he was being treated like a little boy who has used a great deal of enterprise and intelligence to rob a cookie cupboard, and for his pains is sent home with the stolen cookie in his hand.

Vorongil touched his arm. "Come, Bartol," he said gently, "I'm taking you back to the Swiftwing. I don't have to treat you like a prisoner, do I?"

Numbly, Bart gave what the old Lhari asked, his word of honor not to attempt escape (Escape? Where to?) or to attempt to enter the drive chamber of the Swiftwing while they were still among the Lhari worlds.

As they left the council hall, Bart, in a gesture of despair, covered his face with his hands. As he brought them down, he found himself staring at them, transfixed.

The fingers looked longer and thinner than he remembered them, but they were his own hands again. The nails seemed faintly thick and ridged, and there was still a faint grayish tinge through the pale flesh color, but they were human hands. Unmistakably. He felt of his nose and ears, with fumbling fingers; raised his hand and touched the very short, crisp hair growing on his newly shaven skull.

"You fool," said Vorongil to the Mentorian, in disgust, "why didn't you tell him what the medics had done for him? Easy, Bartol!" The old Lhari's arm tightened around his shoulder. "I thought they'd told you. Somebody come here and give the youngster a hand."

Later, in the small cabin (it had been Rugel's) which was to be his prison during the return voyage of the Swiftwing, he had a chance to study his familiar-strange face. He had thought that only a short time—an hour or so—had elapsed between the time he was drugged and the time they took him before the Council. Later, from what he learned about the dispatch schedules of the Swiftwing, he realized that he had been kept under sedation for nearly three weeks, while his face and hands healed.

As Raynor Three had warned, the change was not altogether reversible. Studying his face in the mirror, he could still see a hint of something thin, strange, alien in the set of his features; the nose and chin somewhat too pointed, elfin, to be human. His hands would always be too long, too narrow, too supple. For the rest, he looked grim, older. He could never go back to what he had been before he became a Lhari; it had left its mark on him forever.

Before the Swiftwing lifted, outbound, Vorongil came to his cabin. "You've seen very little of our world," he said diffidently. "I have permission for you to visit the city before we leave Council Spaceport."

"You think you can trust me?" Bart asked bitterly.

Vorongil said gravely, without humor, "The question does not arise. You do not know the coordinates of this world, and have no way of finding them. Within those limitations, you are an honored guest here, and if it would give you any pleasure, you are welcome to see as much of Council Planet as time permits."

It seemed, through Vorongil's kindness, that the old Lhari sensed his bitter defeat. Nothing was to be gained by sulking in his cabin, a prisoner. He had an opportunity which no human, except the Mentorians, had ever had; which perhaps no human would ever have again. He might as well take advantage of it.

Ringg and Meta both seemed startled at his new appearance, but Meta instantly held out her hands, clasping his quickly and warmly. "Bart! I wondered what your real face looked like. But I think I'd have known you anyhow."

Ringg surveyed him wonderingly, shaking his head. "Say something," he implored, "so I'll know you're Bartol."

Bart held out his arm, less gray by the day as the drug wore out of his system. The thin line of the scar was still on it. He raised his forefinger lightly to the fine line on Ringg's cheek. "I couldn't return that now. So let's not get into any more fights."

Ringg laughed and gave him a rough, affectionate shove. "You're Bartol, all right!"

Even his sense of defeat vanished in wonder as they came out into the great spaceport. He saw, now, that the Lhari spaceports in human worlds were built to create, for the spacemen so far from their native worlds, some feeling of home. But everything here was so vast as to stagger the imagination. There were miles and miles of the great ships, lying strewn like pebbles on this monster beachhead into space, bearing the strangeness of a million far-flung stars. He gaped like a child.

Above them, the burning brilliance of a star gave strange glow and color to the crystal pylons. What color was the star? He turned to Meta, irritated at his inability to be sure.

"Meta, what color is this sun? I've been all around the spectrum, and it's not red, blue, green, orange, violet—" He broke off, realizing what he had said and what he had seen. "An eighth color," he finished, anticlimatically.

"You and your talk of colors," Ringg grumbled, "I wish I knew what you Mentorians see! It's like trying to imagine seeing a smell or hearing light!"

Meta laughed. "As far as I know, no one's named it. Sometimes we Mentorians call it catalyst color. I think only Mentorians can see it as separate color."

"So what?" Ringg said impatiently, "What are we going to do, chatter about light waves or see the city?"

Bart acquiesced, trying to sound eager, but a wild excitement was gusting up in him. He dutifully pretended fascination with the towers, the many-leveled roads, the giant dams and pylons, but his thoughts were racing.

The eighth color! There can't be too many suns of this color, or they'd have named it and known it! And telescopes can find it.

Could success be salvaged, then, at the very edge of failure? Maybe he need not go empty-handed, empty-eyed, from the Lhari worlds! They had dismissed him, scornfully, stolen cookie in hand—but maybe it would be a bigger cookie than they dreamed!

The exhilaration lasted through the tour of the port, through the heavy surge of acceleration which brought them up, out and way from Council Planet. Bart, confined in Rugel's cabin, hardly felt like a prisoner, his mind busy with schemes.

I'll study star-maps, and spectroscope reports....

It lasted almost two days of shiptime, and they were readying for Acceleration Two, before he came, figuratively, down to earth. To pick one star out of trillions—and not even in his own galaxy? It would take a lifetime and he didn't even know which of the four or five spiral nebulae in the skies of the human worlds was the Lhari Galaxy. A lifetime? A hundred lifetimes wouldn't do it!

He might have known. If there had been one chance in the odd billion of his making any such discovery, the Lhari would never have given Vorongil permission for the intruder to visit the planet at all. He would have been returned to the Swiftwing as he had been taken from it, by closed car, and imprisoned, maybe even drugged, until he was safely back in the human worlds again.

He was under parole not to enter the drive chamber (and sure he would be stopped if he attempted it anyhow), but when Acceleration One was completed, he went to the viewport in the Recreation Lounge, and nobody threw him out. He stood long, looking at the unfamiliar galaxy of the Lhari stars; the unknown, forever unknowable constellations with their strange shapes. Stars green, gold, topaz, burning blue, sullen red, and the great strangely colored receding sun of the Lhari people, known to them by the melodious name of the Ke Lhiro—which meant, simply, The Sun: it was their first home.

Where had he seen that color? In that stolen glimpse of the Lhari ship landing, long ago? Of all the colors of space, this one he would never know.

He turned away from the unsolvable riddle of the strange constellations; and went to his cabin, to dream of the green star Meristem where he had first plotted known coordinates for a previously unknown world, and to wander in baffling nightmares where he fed jagged, star-colored pieces of hail into the ship's computer and watched them come out as tiny paperdoll spaceships with the letterhead of Eight Colors printed neatly across their sides.

After the warp-drive shift, Vorongil came to his cabin, this time crisp and businesslike.

"We're back in your galaxy," he said, "among the stars you know. We have no passenger space on the Swiftwing; we had to ship out without replacing Rugel, which means we're short two men. I've no authority to ask this of you, but—would you like your old job back for the rest of the voyage?"

Bart glanced at his human hands.

Vorongil shrugged. "We've carried Mentorians as full-ranking Astrogators. There don't happen to be any on the Swiftwing. But there's no law about it."

Bart looked the old Lhari in the eye. "I won't accept Mentorian terms, Vorongil."

"I wouldn't ask it. You worked your way outward on this run, and the High Council didn't see fit to erase those memories or inhibit them. Why should I? Do you want it or not?"

Did he want it? Until this moment Bart had not identified the worst of his pain and defeat—to travel as a passenger, a supercargo, when he had once been part of the Swiftwing. Literally he ached to be back with it again. "I do, rieko mori."

"Very well," Vorongil rapped, "see that you turn out next watch!" He spun round and walked out. His tone was no longer gently indulgent, but sharp and distant. Bart, at first surprised, suddenly understood.

Not now a prisoner, a passenger, a guest on the Swiftwing. He was part of the crew again—and Vorongil was his captain.

The Lhari crew were oddly constrained at first. But Ringg was the same as always, and before long they were almost on the old terms. With every watch, it seemed, he was building a bridge between man and Lhari. They accepted him.

But for what? Something might come, in the far future, of his acceptance, but he wouldn't get the benefit of it. This would be his only voyage; after this he'd be chained again, crawling from planet to planet of a single sun. And as warp-shift followed warp-shift, the Swiftwing retracing the path of her outward cruise star by star, Bart said farewell to them.

One day, at last, he stood at the viewport, watching Procyon Alpha nearing. A year ago, frightened, terribly alone, still unsteady on his new Lhari muscles and terrified by the monsters that were his shipmates, he had watched these planets spinning away. Poor old Rugel, poor old Baldy!

Behind him, Meta came into the lounge.

"Bart—"

He turned to face her. "It won't be much longer, Meta. Tomorrow I'll find out what the Federation is going to do to me. Conspiracy unlawfully to board—and all the rest of it. Even if I don't go to a prison planet, I'll spend the rest of my life chained down to Vega."

"It doesn't have to be that way."

"What other choice is there?" he demanded.

"You're half Mentorian," she said, raising her eager face. "Oh, Bart, you love it so, you know you can't bear to give it up. Stay with us—please stay!"

Before answering, he looked out the viewport a last time. The clouds of cosmic dust swirled and foamed around the familiar jewels of his own sky. Blue, beloved Vega, burning in the heart of the Lyre—home—when would he go home? He had no home now. Yet his father had left him Vega Interplanet, as well as Eight Colors and a quest to the stars.

He searched for the topaz of Sol, where he had learned astrogation; Procyon, where he had become a Lhari; the ruby of Aldebaran (hail and farewell, David Briscoe!); the bloodstone of Antares, where he had learned fear and the shape of integrity. The colors, the unknowable colors of space. And others. Nameless stars where he and his Lhari shipmates had worked and played. And stars he had never seen and would never see, all the endless worlds beyond worlds and stars beyond stars....

He took a last, longing look at the colors of space, then turned his back on them, deliberately giving them up. He could not pay the price the Mentorians paid.

"No, Meta," he said huskily. "The Mentorian way is one way, but—I've had a taste of being one of the masters of space. It's more than most men ever have, maybe it's more than I deserve. But I can't settle for anything less. Not even if it means losing you."

He shut his eyes and stood, head bowed. When he looked up again, he was alone with the stars beyond the viewport, and the lounge was empty.

Chapter Fourteen

The low rainbow building of Eight Colors, near the spaceport of Procyon Alpha, had not changed; and when Bart went in, as he had done a year ago, it seemed that the same varnished girl was sitting before the same glass desk, neon-edged and brittle, with the same chrome-tinged hair and blue fingernails. She looked at Bart in his Lhari clothing, at Meta in her Mentorian robe and cloak, at Ringg, and her unruffled dignity did not turn a hair.

"May I help you?" she inquired, still not caring.

"I want to see Raynor One."

"On what business, please?"

"Tell him," said Bart, with immense satisfaction, "that his boss is here—Bart Steele—and wants to see him right away."

It had a sort of disrupting effect. She seemed to go blurred at the edges. After a minute, blinking carefully, she spoke into the vision-screen, and reported, numbly, "Go on up, Mr. Steele."

He wasn't expecting a welcome. He said so as the elevator rose. "After all, if I'd never come back, he'd doubtless have inherited the whole Eight Colors line, unencumbered. I don't expect he'll be happy to see me. But he's the only one I can turn to."

The elevator stopped, opened. They stepped out, and a man stepped nervously toward them. For a moment, expecting Raynor One, Bart was deceived; then as the man's face spread in a smile of welcome, he stopped in incredulous delight.

"Raynor Three!"

In overflowing gladness, Bart hugged him. It was like a meeting with the dead. He felt as if he had really come home. "But—but you remember me!" he exclaimed, backing away, in amazement.

Slowly, the man nodded. His eyes were grave. "Yes. I decided it wasn't worth it, Bart, to go on losing everything that meant anything to me. Even if it meant I had to give up the stars, never travel again except as a passenger, I couldn't go on being afraid to remember, never knowing the consequences or responsibilities of what I'd done." His sad smile was strangely beautiful.

"The Multiphase sailed without me. I've been here, hoping against hope that someday I'd know the rest."

Associations clicked into place in Bart's mind. The Multiphase. So Raynor Three was the Mentorian who had smuggled David Briscoe off the ship, and whose memories, wrung out by the Lhari captain of that ship, had touched off so many deaths. But he had paid for that—paid many times over. And now must he pay for this, too?

Raynor One strode toward them. "So it's really you. I thought it might be a trap, but Three wouldn't listen. Word came from Antares that Montano had been arrested and his ship confiscated for illegal landing on Lharillis. I thought you were probably dead."

"We sent a boy to do a man's job," Raynor Three said, "and he came back a man. But tell me—" He looked curiously at Ringg and Meta.

Bart introduced them, adding, "I came for help, really. I'm facing charges, and I'm afraid you are, too."

Raynor One said harshly, "A trap, after all, Three! He trapped you, and he's led the Lhari to you!"

"No," Raynor Three said, "or he wouldn't be walking around free and unguarded and with all his memories intact. Tell me about it, Bart." And when Bart had given a quick narration of the Lhari judgment, he nodded, slowly.

"That's all we ever wanted. Don't think you failed, Bart. The horrible part was only the way they were trying to keep it secret."

Ringg interrupted, "Do not judge the Lhari by them, Raynor Three," and Raynor Three said in good Lhari, "I don't, feathertop. Raynors have been working with Lhari since the days of Rhazon of Nedrus. But I wanted an open, official statement of Lhari policy—not secret murders by fanatics. I had confidence in the Lhari as a people, but not in individuals. What good did it do to know that the Lhari council in another galaxy would have condemned the murders and manhunts, when they were going on in this one, day after day?

"Don't you see, Bart?" he continued, "you didn't fail—not if we're going to have the publicity of a test case, publicly heard. That means the Lhari are prepared to admit, before our whole galaxy, that humans can survive warp-drive without cold-sleep. That's all David Briscoe was trying to prove, or your father either—may they rest in peace. So, whatever happens, we've won."

"If you two idealists will give me a minute for cold realities," Raynor One said, "there's this. Among other things. Bart's not yet of legal age. You may not know this, Bart, but your father appointed me your legal guardian. When I turned you over to Three, I'm afraid, I assumed legal responsibility for all the consequences. I ought to have kept you under my own supervision."

Bart smiled at Raynor One's stern face. "I crossed two galaxies, and faced the Lhari High Council, without you to hold my hand. I can face the Trade Federation."

"Naturally I will be responsible for your defense," Raynor One said stiffly.

"But I don't need a defense," Bart said, turning to Raynor Three and meeting his eyes. "I'm going to tell the truth, and let it stand. Don't worry, I'll make sure they don't hold you responsible for my actions."

"Another thing. Some lunatic from Capella arrived here and all but accused me of having you murdered. Do you know a Tommy Kendron?"

"Do I know him!" Bart interrupted with a joyful yell. "Tommy's here? Quick—where do I get in touch with him?"

An hour later they were all gathered at Raynor Three's country house. The talk went on far into the night. Tommy wanted to know everything, and both Raynors wanted to know every detail of Bart's year among the Lhari, while Meta and Ringg were both curious about how it had begun.

Bart tried to forget that the next day might bring trouble, even imprisonment. The Lhari Council had told him to talk as much as he liked about his voyage, and this might be his only chance. When he had finished, Tommy leaned forward and gripped Bart's hand tightly.

"You make them sound like pretty decent people," he said, looking at Ringg. "A year ago, if you'd told me I'd be here with a Lhari spaceman and a bunch of Mentorians, I'd never have believed it."

"Nor I, that I would be as friend under a human roof," Ringg replied. "But a friend to Bart is my friend also." He touched the faint discolored scars on his brow, saying softly, "But for Bart, I would not be here to greet anyone, man or Lhari, as friend."

"So," said Tommy triumphantly, "you haven't failed, even if you didn't discover the secret of the Eighth Color—"

But a sudden, blinding light burst over Bart as Ringg moved his hand to the scars. Once again he searched a cave beneath a green star, where Ringg lay unconscious and bleeding, and played his Lhari light fearfully over a waterfall of colored minerals. And there was one whose color he could not identify—red, blue, violet, green, none of these—the color of an unknown star in an unknown galaxy, the shimmer of a landing Lhari ship, the color of an unknown element in an unknown fuel—

"The secret of the Eighth Color," he said, and stood up, his hands literally shaking in excitement. "I'm an idiot! No, don't ask me any questions! I could still be wrong. But even if I go to a prison planet, the Eighth Color isn't a secret any more!"

When the others had gone back to the city, he sat with Raynor Three in the room where the latter had told him of his father's death, where he had first seen his terrifying Lhari face. They spoke little, but Raynor Three finally asked, "Were you serious about not wanting a defense, Bart?"

"I was. All I want is a chance to tell my own story in my own way. Where everyone will hear me."

Raynor Three looked at him curiously. "There's something you're not telling, Bart. Want to tell me?"

Bart hesitated, then held out his hand and clasped his kinsman's. "Thanks—but no."

Raynor Three saw his hesitation and chuckled. "All right, son. Forget I asked. You've grown up."

It was good to sleep in a soft human-type bed again, to eat breakfast and shave and dress in ordinary human clothing again. But Bart folded his Lhari tights and the cloak tenderly, with regret. They were the memory of an experience no one else would ever have.

Raynor Three let him take the controls as they flew back to the spaceport city; and a little before noon they entered the great crystal pylon that was the headquarters of the Federation Trade Bureau on Procyon Alpha. Men and Lhari were moving in the lobby; among them Bart saw Vorongil, Meta at his side. He smiled at her, received a wan smile in return.

Would Vorongil feel that Bart had deceived him, betrayed him, when he heard Bart today?

In the hearing room, four white-crested Lhari sat across from four dignified, well-dressed men, representatives of the Federation of Intergalactic Trade. The space beyond was wholly filled with people, crowded together, and carrying stereo cameras, intercom equipment, the creepie-peepie of the on-the-spot space commentator.

"Mr. Steele, we had hoped to make this a quiet hearing, without undue publicity. But we cannot deny the news media the privilege of covering it, unless you wish to claim the right to privacy."

"No, indeed," Bart said clearly. "I want them all to hear what I'm going to say."

Raynor One came up to the bench. "Bart, as your guardian, I advise against it. Some people will call this a publicity stunt. It won't do Eight Colors any good to admit that men have been spying on the Lhari—"

"I want press coverage," Bart repeated stubbornly, "and as many star-systems on the relay as possible."

"All right. But I wash my hands of it," Raynor One said angrily.

Bart told his story simply: his meeting with the elder Briscoe, his meeting with Raynor One—carefully not implicating Raynor One in the plot—Raynor Three's work in altering his appearance to that of a Lhari, and the major events of his cruise on the Swiftwing. When he came to the account of the shift into warp-drive, he saw the faces of the press reporters, and realized that for them this was the story of the year—or century: humans can endure star-drive! But he went on, not soft-pedaling Montano's attempted murder, his own choice, the trip to the Lhari world—

One of the board representatives interrupted testily, "What is the point of this lengthy narrative? You can give the story to the newsmen without our official sanction, if you want to make it a heroic epic, young Steele. We have heard sufficient to prove your guilt, and that of Raynor, in the violation of treaty—"

"Nevertheless, I want this official," Bart said. "I don't want to be mobbed when they hear that I have the secret of the star-drive."

The effect was electric. The four Lhari sat up; their white crests twitched. Vorongil stared, his gray eyes darkening with fear. One of the Lhari leaned forward, shooting the question at him harshly.

"You did not discover the coordinates of the Council Planet of Ke Lhiro! You did not discover—"

"I did not," Bart said quietly. "I don't know them and I have no intention of trying to find them. We don't need to go to the Lhari Galaxy to find the mineral that generates the warp-frequencies, that they call 'Catalyst A' and that the Mentorians call the 'Eighth Color.' There is a green star called Meristem, and a spectroscopic analysis of that star, I'm sure, will reveal what unknown elements it contains, and perhaps locate other stars with that element. There must be others in our galaxy, but the coordinates of the star Meristem are known to me."

Vorongil was staring at him, his mouth open. He leaped up and cried out, shaking, "But they assured us that among your memories—there was nothing of danger to us—"

Compassionately, gently, Bart said, "There wasn't—not that they knew about, Vorongil. I didn't realize it myself. I might never have remembered seeing a mineral that was of a color not found in the spectrum. Certainly, a memory like that meant nothing to the Lhari medics who emptied out my mind and turned over all my thoughts. You Lhari can't see color at all.

"So no one but I saw the color of the mineral in the cave; you Lhari yourselves don't know that your fuel looks unlike anything else in the universe. You never cared to find out how your world looked to your Mentorians. So your medics never questioned my memories of an eighth color. To you, it's just another shade of gray, but under a light strong enough to blind any but Mentorian eyes, it takes on a special color—"

The conference broke up in disorder, the four Lhari clustering together in a furious babble, then hastily leaving the room. Bart stood waiting, feeling empty and cold. Vorongil's stare baffled him with unreadable emotion.

"You fool, you unspeakable young idiot!" Raynor One groaned. "Why did you blurt it out like that before every news media in the galaxy? Why, we could have had a monopoly on the star-drive—Eight Colors and Vega Interplanet!" As he saw the men of the press approaching with their microphones, lights, cameras and TV equipment, he gripped Bart urgently by the arm.

"We can still salvage something! Don't talk any more! Refer them to me—say I'm your guardian and your business manager—you can still make something of this—"

"That's just what I don't want to do," Bart replied, and broke away from him to approach the newsmen.

"Yes, certainly, I'll answer all your questions, gentlemen."

Raynor One flung up his hands in despair, but over their shoulder he saw the glowing face of Meta, and smiled. She, at least, would understand. So would Raynor Three.

A page boy touched Bart on the arm. "Mr. Steele," he said, "you are to appear immediately before the World Council!"

He was to be asked one question again and again in the days that followed, but his real answer was to Meta and Raynor Three, looking quietly past Raynor One and speaking to the news cameras that would carry his words all over the galaxy to men and Lhari:

"Why didn't I keep it for myself? Because there are always men like Montano, who in their mistaken pride will murder and steal for such things. I want this knowledge to be open to all men, to be used for their benefit. There has been too much secrecy already. I want all men to have the stars."

He had to tell his story again and again to the hastily summoned representatives of the Galactic Federation. At one point the delegate from his home star of Vega actually rose and shouted to him, "This is treason! You betrayed your home world—and the whole human race! Don't you know the Lhari may fight a war over this?"

Bart remembered Vorongil's silent, sad confession of the Lhari fears.

"No," he said gently. "No. There won't be any war unless we start one. The Lhari won't start any war. Believe me."

But inwardly, he sweated. What would the Lhari do?

They had to wait for representatives of the Lhari Council to make the journey from their home galaxy; meanwhile they kept Bart in protective custody. There was, of course, no question of sending him to a "prison planet"; public opinion would have crucified any government that suggested punishment for the man who had discovered a human world with deposits of Catalyst A. Bart could claim an "explorer's share," and Raynor One had lost no time in filing that claim on his behalf.

But he was lonely and anxious. They had confined him to a set of rooms high in the building overlooking the spaceport; from the balcony he could see the ships landing and departing. Life went on, ships came and went, and out there in the vast night of space, the suns and colors flamed and rolled, heedless of the little atoms that traveled and intrigued between them.

A night came when the buzzer sounded and he opened the door to Raynor One and Raynor Three.

"Better turn on your vision-screen, Bart. The Elder of the Lhari Council has arrived with their official decision, and he's going to announce it."

Bart waited, anxiously, pacing the room, while on the TV screen various dignitaries presented the Elder.

"We are the first race to travel the stars." A bald head, an ancient Lhari face seamed like glazed pottery, looked at Bart from the screen, and Bart remembered when he had stood before that face, sick with defeat. But now he need not pretend to hold his head erect.

"We have had a long and triumphant time as masters of the stars," the Lhari said. "But triumph and power will sicken and stagnate the race which holds them too long unchallenged. We reached this point once before. Then a Lhari captain, Rhazon of Nedrun, abandoned the safe ways of caution, and out of his blind leap in the blind dark came many good things. Trade with the human race. Our Mentorian allies. A system of mathematics to take the hazards from our star-travel.

"Yet once again the Lhari had grown cautious and fearful. And a young man named Bartol took a blind leap into unknown darkness, all alone—"

"Not alone," Bart said as if to himself, "it took two men called Briscoe. And my father. And a couple of Raynors. And even a man called Montano, because without that, I'd never have decided—"

"Like Rhazon of Nedrun, like all pioneers, this young man has been cursed by his own people, the very ones who will one day benefit from his daring. He has found his people a firm footing among the stars. It is too late for the Lhari to regret that we did not sooner extend you the hand of welcome there. You have climbed, unaided, to join us. For good or ill, we must make room for you.

"But there is room for all. Competition is the lifeblood of trade, and we face the future without fear, knowing that life still holds many surprises for the living. I say to you: welcome to the stars."

Even while Bart stood speechless with the knowledge of success, the door opened again, and Bart, turning, cried out in amazement.

"Tommy! Ringg! Meta!"

"Sure," Tommy exclaimed, "we've got to celebrate," but Bart stopped, looking past them.

"Captain Vorongil!" he said, and went to greet the old Lhari. "I thought you'd hate me, rieko mori." The term of respect fell naturally from his lips.

"I did, for a time," Vorongil said quietly. "But I remembered the day we stood on Lharillis, by the monument. And that you risked—perhaps your life, certainly your eyesight—to save us from death. So when the Elder asked for my estimate of your people, I gave it."

"I thought it sounded like you." Bart felt that his happiness was complete.

"And now," Ringg cried, "let's celebrate! Meta, you haven't even told him that he's free!"

But while the party got rolling, Bart wondered—free for what? And after a little while he went out on the balcony and stood looking down at the spaceport, where the Swiftwing lay in shadow, huge, beloved—renounced.

"What now, Bartol?" Vorongil's quiet voice asked from his elbow. "You're famous—notorious. You're going to be rich, and a celebrity."

"I was wishing I could get away until the excitement dies down."

"Well," said Vorongil, "why don't you? The Swiftwing ships out tonight, Bartol—for Antares and beyond. It will be a couple of years before your Eight Colors can be made over into an Interstellar line—and as Raynor One has said to me several times, he'll have to handle all those details, for you're not of age yet.

"I've been thinking. Now that we Lhari must share space with your people, you'll need experienced men for your ships. Unless we all want the disasters born of trial and error, we Lhari had better help you train your men quickly and well. I want you to go back on the Swiftwing with me. Not an apprentice, but representative of Eight Colors, to act as liaison between men and Lhari—at least until your own affairs claim your attention."

Behind them on the balcony, Tommy appeared, making signals to Bart: "Say yes! Say yes, Bart! I did!"

Bart's eyes suddenly filled. Out of defeat he had won success beyond his greatest hopes. But he did not feel all glad; he felt only a heavy responsibility. Whether good or bad came of the gift he had snatched from the stars, would rest in large measure on his own shoulders. He was going back to space—to learn the responsibility that went with it.

"I accept," he said gravely.

"Oh, boy!" Tommy dragged Ringg into a sort of war dance of exuberant celebration, pointing at the flaring glow of the spaceport gates. "Here, by grace of the Lhari, stands the doorway to all the stars," he quoted. "Well, maybe you were here first. But look out—we're coming!"

A doorway to the stars. Bart had crossed that doorway once, frightened and alone. Dad, if you could only know! The first interstellar ship of Eight Colors was to bear the name Rupert Steele, but that was years in the future.

Now, looking at the Swiftwing, at Ringg and Tommy, at Raynor Three and Vorongil, who would all be his shipmates in the new world they were building, he felt suddenly very lonely again.

"Come in, Bart. It's your party," Meta said softly, and he felt her hand lying in his. He looked down at the pretty Mentorian girl. She would be with him, too. And suddenly he knew he would never be lonely again.

His arm around Meta, his friends—man and Lhari—at his shoulder, he went back to the celebration, to plan for the first intergalactic voyage to the stars.